ALMOST VISIBLE

ALMOST VISIBLE

A Novel

MICHELLE SINCLAIR

Baraka
Books

Montréal

ISBN 978-1-77186-294-3 pbk; 978-1-77186-308-7 epub; 978-1-77186-309-4 pdf
Cover by Lucia Granados
Book Design by Folio Infographie
Editing and proofreading: Elise Moser, Robin Philpot, Blossom Thom

Legal Deposit, 3rd quarter 2022
Bibliothèque et Archives nationales du Québec
Library and Archives Canada

Published by Baraka Books of Montreal

Printed and bound in Quebec

TRADE DISTRIBUTION & RETURNS
Canada – UTP Distribution: UTPdistribution.com

UNITED STATES
Independent Publishers Group: IPGbook.com

We acknowledge the support from the Société de développement des entreprises culturelles (SODEC) and the Government of Quebec tax credit for book publishing administered by SODEC.

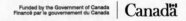

For my mum, Joy

"To love purely is to consent to distance, it is to adore the distance between ourselves and that which we love."

Simone Weil

Fin.

Her eyes are covered, so she relies on her ears. Loud, metallic sounds do not drown out the constant hum, nor the piercing voices. They laugh when she says her name is Bárbara. They say, you no longer exist. When the men brought her to the building near the sea, she could sense it, hard hands stripped and searched her. Rough, greedy handfuls of her flesh. Bárbara thinks about her mother's soft skin like satin. Her mother, who will have to grieve for a child and a grandchild.

She was leaving the apartment. They were waiting outside the door, but she hadn't seen them until they came up behind her, placing their arms under hers, lifting her up and tossing her into the car like a child. It all happened so naturally, it seemed as though it was routine and she'd just forgotten.

The last time he saw her, Andrés had recited a poem for her—frantically, out of breath—as though he knew his time was running out:

> *te nombraré veces y veces.*
> *me acostaré con vos noche y día.*
> *noches y días con vos.*
> *me ensuciaré cogiendo con tu sombra.*

He hadn't known about the child. Or had he? He'd been so strange, of late. As though his soul were slowly scattering to the wind like desiccated leaves until his body disappeared too. She hadn't seen him for weeks, and hadn't had time to tell him about the baby.

They remove her hood and push her inside—the ceiling too low to stand up straight, the bed too short to stretch out fully. A fluorescent light penetrates and illuminates everything, including grey walls and black twin beds. A woman is curled up on one of the beds, arms folded over her head like tulip petals, purple marks on her arms and legs. The men tell Bárbara to write a letter to her mother. They tell her to lie, to say the other side captured her. She imagines her mother sitting on her bed, tracing her handwriting, crying with relief.

Someone asks her name. The voice is so quiet. It is the woman on the other bed. Bárbara turns her head, her ears ringing, towards the voice and answers. The woman repeats her name a few times, as though memorizing it. Bárbara. Bárbara. Then she says her name, María. María de los Ángeles. María asks how old she is. Bárbara tells her, "I am twenty-two. I live in Flores."

María says, "Never forget it. Never say it in the past tense."

Lying curled in her bed, her body dirty and aching, she hears a murmur like the song of trees when they speak to one another through the wind. Bárbara thinks at first that the others are praying—*Josefa, Luis, Ana, Marco, María, Bárbara*—names whispered over and over so they will not forget. This way, no one will disappear.

One guard takes a special interest in her. He has read her articles. He says, "You wrote that parallel lines never meet, and that can't be contradicted by Euclidean geometry. But what about elliptic geometry? Sometimes the relative might seem subjective, depending on your experience. Sometimes, the truth is none other than where you happen to be standing."

She doesn't answer. He thinks he is helping her.

"It doesn't need to be difficult. Minds can change," he says.

Her mind doesn't change, though they are persuasive. Unflinching. She gives birth to her baby blindfolded, and they take the baby away. A few hours later, someone enters the room and places a bundled weight into her arms. A nurse tells her to feed it. She and the baby are ravenous for one another. She caresses and smells and whispers to the baby with a desperation she does not recognize, to absorb and convey as much as she can. She had wanted to show her baby all the beauty in the world.

She senses her baby's gentle acceptance and trust—the understanding of the newly born. The baby has not yet shed the wisdom of the womb. The nurse leans in and tells her quietly that the baby is a girl. Bárbara nods and stifles a cry. She tells the nurse that her baby's name is Clara.

She never sees her again. Bárbara will live, for a short time longer, with the phantom weight of a bundle in her arms.

She sees only the distance between herself and all that she loves.

PART I

LIFTING ANCHOR

Chapter 1

Tess is passing through.

This is what she tells herself when she arrives in the new city. Though she doesn't know it yet, all that she will learn to love and hate about big cities will belong to her. Congestion and construction, graffiti and grit, museums and metros. The city has enough self-assurance that it is not cliché, and Tess won't be either.

This is what she tells herself.

Tess's new apartment, the one she shares with Jana, is located on the edge of the Portuguese quarter. Statues of Jesus and Mary grace the tiny, fenced-in grass plots that push up against the sidewalks. Every fence and pole in the city has a bike leaning against it. Kids play in the hidden alleys, running behind wooden fences and through parks as though they were the first kids in the world to do so. Evidence of history's craftsmanship— the wear and tear of time, careless tenants, huge families and unforgiving weather—like small acts of love.

Amongst the houses are scattered colossal Catholic churches; old factories with family surnames still painted on the rough, blood-red brick; smoked-meat-sandwich shops; milkshake diners and family-owned shoe stores. They're still there, in different states of disrepair, resolutely relevant, and not yet relegated to the past. The city breathes, and people are strolling and eating ice cream. Warehouses, docks, freight yards and distilleries are familiar to Tess, but not on this scale. She has gone back in time, yet she's moving forwards. It feels like a carnival every day—a gritty one, fun if somewhat frightening, and she loves its shabby elegance.

She wonders if her lonely heart could be cured by the city and all the strangers living their lives, so close by.

Tess has never lived in a big city. She marvels at the construction—the mission to grow and improve and be a modern city in motion, which at times serves to excavate the past. The discovery of ancient artifacts—those dormant, silent witnesses to the amnesia of the present as shoppers pound the pavement for back-to-school sales—could, for some, usher in a sense of an ending. For some it may represent a juncture. In the glass of the new buildings, Tess makes out reflections of the old brick ones.

She likes to watch the ancient men as they sit on park benches in plazas discussing the old country, and pretty women riding bicycles with scarves trailing behind them like a promise. She likes greeting the homeless man who sleeps in the doorway of the bank, or smiling at the self-conscious teens on Ste. Catherine with their gym bags and energy drinks. There is enough strange somehow, to offset the familiar. Everywhere a story or an image.

She feels a delighted, drunken disorientation, and decides to be a flâneuse. She waits on a bench on Boulevard St. Laurent for a bus she doesn't board. She watches families on Mont Royal unpack their picnics in the park. She studies university students with backpacks and ponytails as they're guided in groups through orientation.

Only a few men proposition her, and one exposes himself from the bushes.

It may explain why being a flâneur is a pastime largely reserved for men. She'll put up with a penis pointed at her like a pistol if it means she can witness other lives in real time. If she can be, for a moment, tethered to another mind. She marvels at the ways we find protection in one another, and from one another. Do we feel safer surrounded by millions of people? And yet, we build fences. She's overcome by an unreasonable affection for strangers. She never feels lonely, though she is almost always alone.

She grew up in the woods surrounding an old farmhouse with a haunted attic. She fantasized about mysteries only she could solve.

When she wasn't daydreaming about saving the world, she watched. She watched birds emerge from their shells, shivering and wet. She cried if someone looked at dandelions the wrong way. She watched the ocean toss and turn, and she'd watch her mother. Her mother was the true mystery. Her mother was full of wonder, but suppressed her curiosity under a tight smile and a sigh. Tess witnessed it, from time to time, in the way her mother would reach out occasionally, as though to touch her.

A few months prior, Tess had written to Jana for information about the city. She wanted to let Jana know of her intentions to move, and asked her for advice about renting a small apartment. She said she needed a fresh start and a job. She didn't know if Jana would remember her and almost hoped she wouldn't, but Jana responded immediately and generously.

She had an extra room and would *love love love* to have an "old friend" stay with her.

When she'd first seen Jana's stone building with its delicate black spiralling staircase, she'd been taken aback. So elegant. She had grown up enveloped by the Maritime mist, taking its grace for granted, and hadn't anticipated the effect of the city on her senses. Tess wasn't used to the way one could lose their bearings in an urban setting; how she could be catapulted to distant shores in her mind—by customs and cultures imported from all corners of the world, a kaleidoscope of colours, sounds, textures and smells, each one in turn making her feel she'd travelled farther than she had.

As though she'd crossed oceans, or left herself behind.

She decided she would belong. The city was sweet, harsh, paradoxical, and full of voices, drowning out her own. A relief, really.

Tess places her foot on the first step—one hand on her suitcase and the other on the handrail. As she climbs, the geraniums judge her from their hanging pots. Three flights. The door of each apartment is painted a different colour. The staircase shakes a little and she thinks she might slip off backwards. Her body sends out distress signals. Her hair feels unclean. She wonders how she'll manage not to die when the stairs are covered in snow and ice. If she can stay until the winter. If she doesn't overstay her welcome.

Jana's apartment is on the top floor and her door is painted purple. She's dressed in a white bathrobe, her long wet curls stretching over her shoulders, falling onto her breasts. Droplets of water sit on her chest. She looks almost the same as she had in high school, with a mane of curly dark hair and wide eyes. It seems she hasn't aged at all—just grown into the person she was meant to be. Tess wraps her arms around her body and stutters until Jana leans forward.

"Tess? It's you! My God, you're so beautiful."

Jana's voice is the same as Tess remembers—hoarse, almost male. It inspires trust and longing at the same time. Tess has a flashback of Jana at a party in high school, when she turned up the volume of the stereo and covered her ears. Tess thought that perhaps Jana's will was at odds with her needs. The limits of her self had not yet been defined, or she was ignoring them.

Jana has the same mannerisms as before. Something in the movement of her shoulders, in the way she tilts her chin. How can a person be the same, yet so changed? Or so changed, yet the same? The lines of Jana's adult body remind Tess of sand dunes on a beach—soft, firm, and inviting. Tess has to repress an unexpected desire to embrace her. She also represses the desire to ask Jana what she means. Had she not been beautiful before?

Of course she hadn't. But then again, her mother always admonished her for worrying about people's opinions.

No business of hers trying to guess what people are thinking.

Jana was popular, collecting friends, where Tess had exactly one. Tess hadn't needed anyone other than Astrid, until Jana invited her to a pool party. It was eleventh grade. Tess didn't have the right bathing suit. All the other girls wore bikinis, and she had an old navy-blue one-piece that hadn't fit her properly for years. She didn't know what to do with her body and stood around with her arms covering her stomach. Barely anyone spoke to her.

Tess remembered almost everything from eleventh grade. She remembered the name of her gym teacher, and what she and Astrid talked about each day as they walked home together.

She remembered how Astrid was rebellious but not because she was insecure; she simply wanted to be herself.

Moments from Jana's party stood out, too. In later years, when she thought of adolescence, she was carried back to this. Nothing ever seemed to her as perfect as that moment, sitting on the edge of the pool, a cold glass of spiked lemonade in her hand as she contemplated her ankles and feet moving through the water, which created prisms and shadows and reflections too bright for her naked eyes.

Tess felt the soft afternoon sun on her skin. She was backlit and beautiful, and as she looked over at the other kids, she realized Jana was smiling at her. Acceptance. The young, shiny bodies around her moved in and out of her line of vision, some in the water, some on the edge of the snack table. They moved past one another, touched arms, whispered, pushed. They giggled and laughed. It was choreography. A show. And Tess was part of it.

In that moment, her two desires—the pursuits of beauty and belonging—had blended. She couldn't have known that this flash of a moment would become her baseline for happiness. She had discovered sensation, strong enough to satiate. She was young enough to believe that her unresolved longing had finally abated and her desires had been met. A joking tussle broke out then and someone was pushed into the water. The intensity of the moment burst. Tess dipped herself slowly into the cool water until she reached the bottom of the pool and sat still for a moment, cross-legged, in the aquatic silence that muffled the din outside, holding her breath and squeezing shut her eyes.

It occurred to Tess that Jana may have invited her to the party to be kind, but cool kids couldn't be qualified with such simple definitions. There had to be more to it. Their popularity was proof that they were interesting. Tess made a hobby of studying them, like an anthropologist, to understand what made them tick.

But she didn't know how to reconcile the need for acceptance with her desire to retain her sense of self. She found it difficult to unlearn all she considered true.

Her life wasn't all sad. There had been other moments worthy of reminiscence—open windows and sunlight, board games, loving pets and meals outdoors, lanterns and light. Still, if someone had asked her to describe her youth, she might have said she felt like a ship in a storm, crashing through rolling waves, yet always within view of the horizon. A seasick kind of hope. And nothing much has changed.

Chapter 2

Jana invites her to come in. The inside of the apartment is long and narrow and leads into a living room and a kitchen, with two bedrooms off the kitchen. Some of the walls are painted in dark colours—forest green, maroon, or navy blue. Statement walls. The rest of the walls are a sparkling white.

In the living room, beanbag chairs are strewn about a Persian rug. Candles and books line the shelves, and plants seem to fill every other possible space. Jana has a stereo where one would ordinarily find a TV. Next to this are stacks of cassette tapes.

Tess learns that Jana listens only to mixtapes made by other people. Like auditory love letters, she says. A few tapes of mostly wordless, haunting Pakistani music to remind her of her grandmother; recordings of rain, waterfalls, and the howls of wolves for relaxation; grunge bands from the '90s from an ex.

Jana's black hair hangs gold at the ends and her fingernails sparkle with a bright purple shine. Tess has dirt under her nails.

Tiny lights are strung up in the kitchen, and the air has a soft, yellow glow. From their vase on the wooden dining table, tulips nod their large purple heads.

"I bought these to celebrate your arrival," Jana says. Tess's throat closes up. Jana bought flowers for her. She hadn't thought to bring anything, so certain had she been that this arrangement wouldn't work. Perhaps she can sneak out to buy Jana a bottle of wine.

A tiny balcony hangs off the kitchen. A table covered in succulents and orange gerbera flowers is just big enough to tuck in two folding chairs. The spare room is on the other side of the kitchen. A tiny room. A closet really, facing a brick wall, but Tess is overcome with gratitude when she sees the single bed and desk, and another vase with pink tulips.

The room seems full. Though the plants in their terracotta pots are artfully positioned, Jana seems to have forgotten to water these. They look dry. This is a comforting sign—Jana isn't perfect.

Jana is theatrical and generous as she shows Tess around, and Tess finds herself speaking louder than usual to match Jana's inflections and enthusiasm. She stands too close to Jana. She almost knocks over a cup. Tess wonders what kind of first impression she's making, though it can't be a first impression if they knew one another before, can it? It is an impression layered with perceptions from the past. Tess wants to distance herself from Jana's prejudices. She feels hopeful and insecure at once. She is overcome with gratitude laced with shame. And how will she ever pay her back?

But Jana has enough money to keep buying plants, and to let Tess live in the apartment rent-free until she finds a job.

"You'll be doing me a favour," Jana says. "I made the mistake of letting this guy, Robert, live here for a while, but he had no intention of finding a job. He drank all my beer. I was finally able to throw him out because you were coming."

Jana puts the kettle on. Tess decides she can help to keep the plants alive. She makes a mental note not to drink Jana's beer.

"Why did you decide to move?" Jana asks.

Ten hours in a car by herself should have provided her enough time to prepare an answer to that very question, but she wasn't used to being asked about her choices.

Back home, when she sold most of her belongings, packed her winter jacket and hiking boots, and scrubbed her little house, it felt good to finally take action. She said goodbye to her father and co-workers. She had a tearful farewell dinner at the pub with Astrid, who said Tess would be home in no time.

"You'll miss me too much," Astrid said, lifting her pint to her lips, her dark eyes glowing behind her glasses. She'd taken to braiding her hair recently. They'd grabbed one of the booths near the stage, barely able to hear one another over the sound of guitars and fiddles, and sat close together so they wouldn't have to shout. Astrid was the closest thing Tess had to a sister, and Tess could tell she was upset. Astrid even intimated that Tess might be avoiding reality. Whatever that might be.

Just because everyone else was marrying and having children didn't mean Tess had to stay and watch. It wasn't original, what she was doing, but she told Astrid that it felt right.

"Then that settles it, I suppose," Astrid had said.

Tess had thought about Astrid as she'd driven northwest, with the harbour in her rear-view mirror. She revisited their conversations as she passed through quaint towns and roadside blueberry pie stands.

The most difficult part was her father's sad confusion over her sudden decision to leave, which she couldn't explain or justify. She hoped he'd understand that there was some gossamer-fine connection to her mother's recent death. But how could she leave him when he was so lonely? He'd been such a good dad.

She remembered when he used to hold his hand over her tiny belly, she must have been about five or six, and pretend his hand was a spider. The "spider" walked all over her, tap dancing and tickling. She laughed until she cried. Once, she was so riled up, she took the spider's "legs" in her hands and bent them backwards.

Her father had cried out in shock, and it scared her. Regaining composure, he pretended to cry for the spider who had "died." Later on, she remembered layers of pain from that moment. She'd disappointed her father with her ferocity. She'd even hurt him. She also believed that she had, in fact, killed the spider. She'd shown no empathy or compassion. When she cried herself to sleep later on, it was as much for the spider as for herself. It seemed she'd failed some important test.

Now her dad asked her why she was moving if she didn't have a job, or a program of study, or even the prospect of a romantic liaison. If she had one of these, then he would understand—fate would be in charge. She didn't know how to explain that she was tired of waiting. Whatever happened now would result from her own decisions.

She might need to figure out who she could blame. Like grief, perhaps. Or capitalism. Or her own stupidity.

She hadn't considered the width of New Brunswick, and had forgotten the trees. She was tired. She'd imagined parking her car on the side of the road, leaving behind her trunk full of crap, and running into the forest. She could live by her wits alone: sleeping, drinking, and eating in the woods—all she needed for survival—her body growing hairy, her language becoming her own. She'd haunt the hunters and loggers, soaring about the trees like a wisp of smoke, a flash of shadows—surprising, teasing, and frightening them. She could emerge as a legend.

She could imagine no better end.

In the car, she slept with her eyes open, as her mother used to say. She made herself notice details to stay awake: cream-coloured bungalows, garden gnomes, and purple flowers on obscenely well-watered lawns. She rolled down the windows. Her hair flew around her face and she felt glamorous for a moment. She had nothing to lose. Her radio was broken, so she sang and accompanied herself with percussion on the steering wheel: Patsy Cline. Johnny Cash. Nat King Cole. Her mother's old favourites. The songs she had sung when she'd thought she was alone.

Occasionally Tess drove past a house and barn with horses or cows nearby. Their tails flicked at flies like metronomes. The rhythm of the summer.

She hadn't realized she'd crossed the border into Québec until she saw the sign for Saint-Louis-du-Ha! Ha! She slowed until she'd stopped on the side of the highway. A truck rolled past, but otherwise the highway was empty. She got out of her car and stretched, looking east, looking west. No turning back now. She was really on her way. This was not a summer road trip with her parents, like the first time they'd laughed at that town's name, imagining it to be full of clowns and comedians; it was a deliberate and unquestionable choice.

Tess wanted to believe in the possibility of a new start.

Jana shares her stir-fry with Tess, and they drink beer in front of an open window. The humidity is occasionally swept away by a flirty breeze, which tickles the back of Tess's neck. She's happy to watch Jana.

"So, what's the news back home?" Jana asks, an expert with chopsticks.

"Everyone's proud that you're a big shot," Tess says.

Shit. That sounds like she's belittling Jana's accomplishments.

"So, I want to hear all the details."

"I bet. Back home, anyone who moves away thinks they're a big shot by definition, right?" Jana says.

Tess nods.

"So, what's your plan now?" Jana asks.

Tess wishes she'd stop asking questions.

"Are you trying to stress me out?" Tess asks.

"Not at all, I just want to see if I can help," Jana answers, taken aback. Tess had meant it as a joke, but as usual it hadn't come out properly.

"I'm sorry. I'm just not sure what I'm going to do. I have a degree in social work, but never worked as a social worker. I became a dental assistant," Tess says.

She talks about teeth, and about how much she loves helping people.

So stupid.

Jana's art is being commissioned all around the city, she's managing collectives and organizing festivals, and Tess says she wants to "help people"?

Tess doesn't know what she wants. She wants to see patterns and to regain control. She wants to outsmart the unpredictable and reorder her life, before life can do it for her. To deny herself and distract herself. She wants to find traces of her mother.

"My mum died last year. I thought a change of scenery might be good for me."

"Oh, Tess, I'm so sorry."

Tess smiles, mostly to reassure Jana, and takes a long swig of beer.

"I can probably connect you to some people here to help you find a job. My friend Béatrice works at Meals on Wheels, and I think they were hiring," Jana says.

"Thanks. That would be great," Tess says. She's not convincing.

Jana keeps her eyes steadily on Tess.

"Just so odd. Seeing you sitting here in my living room," Jana says.

"Why?"

"It's hard to explain," Jana says, as she stands. She heads to the kitchen.

"I remind you of everything we wanted to escape," Tess says, quietly.

Jana doesn't seem to have heard. She returns with a bottle of Scotch and pours two glasses without asking.

"I'm not sure how to put it. Seeing you makes me wonder which version of us is the real one. The one in my memory, or the one sitting here in my living room. I mean, you seem so different."

Tess spins her Scotch glass slowly in the palm of her hand.

"How am I different?" Tess asks.

"Hard to say. It's more of a feeling I get, as opposed to anything I could describe. Like, I can't pinpoint it. But I guess we didn't really know one another that well."

"The problem with memory," Tess says, a bit tipsy, "is that we look back at ourselves as though we were different people. We're embarrassed of our motivations, so we invent new ones to protect ourselves from the truth of the moment."

Jana nods, looks at her phone, and looks back at Tess.

"You know, as an artist, I try to understand memory. Like, how do people interpret and express their own love and pain? But then, I am interpreting their interpretations. Does my own empathy cast a shadow on their memories? Do I project my own stuff?" Jana asks.

"Is empathy even a real thing?" Tess says.

Jana laughs, as though Tess was trying to make a joke.

"Do you remember what happened at my pool party?" Jana asks.

Out of nowhere, a small, thin cat jumps onto Tess's lap, its claws entering the tops of her thighs.

"Ingrid! Where did you come from?" Jana laughs.

Tess tentatively pats the soft grey cat.

"You don't have allergies, right? Humphrey was my other cat. He passed away last year," Jana says, checking her phone for photos of Humphrey. "Now it's just us girls." Tess will have to bring the conversation back to the party at another time.

What had happened at the pool party for Tess—other than a fleeting moment, which would forever define happiness, and a descent into a long, drawn-out affair with alcohol?

What does Jana remember?

Tess had admired Jana. Had even wanted to be her. This seems now an unforgivable weakness. Maybe now, she could start to see the world through Jana's eyes. Jana could be a funhouse mirror and throw Tess's image back—distorted, but polished. Could she rewrite her understanding of her past in her mind? Could retrospect afford her that nuance? Tess likes how she feels in Jana's apartment. She likes how she feels with Jana. She likes how she feels, now that she's had a few drinks.

It occurs to Tess that Jana is the kind of woman her mother would have wanted as a daughter. She tries to relax. She admires the photos of Ingrid and Humphrey curled up around one another's bodies, yin and yang, but she wonders what Jana meant. Now she is heavy and wants to sink into a more comfortable chair. She holds her glass in front of her eye, and sees Jana in the light. Blurrier. Sepia. Like an old photo.

Ingrid readjusts herself on Tess's lap—little pricks of her skin—and the cat curves and lifts her back to stretch out her thin, flexible spine.

After a glass or two, nostalgia settles in like fog. They revisit memories that never would have been considered favourites but for the fact that they are mutual, safe, and securely resigned to the past. For example, Andy's parents' bowling alley, where they'd each, at respective times, had too much to drink and made out with Andy. Then regretted it.

When Jana has enough of Scotch and reminiscing, Tess pretends she has too. She watches Jana go about what she assumes is her nightly routine: rinsing glasses, locking the front door, shutting off the lights. Tess follows her around, offering to help. Unsure. She brushes her teeth for the first time in Jana's bathroom, which is also her own, taking care not to leave white spots on the mirror. She washes her face and wipes off the counter. She opens a cupboard and sees white towels, rolled up and placed in a pyramid shape.

Tess wants to ask Jana if she knew Cam. Most people knew of him, even if they didn't have a personal connection. He was involved in everything. He was the person people turned to for help. He told her that everyone is good, because all they want is to be loved. She thought this was just something to say to be impressive, but when she was with him, Tess felt as though she understood. It was simple. Still, caring about people as much as they deserve would be dangerous for her health.

Jana asks if she needs anything else, and they say goodnight. For a dizzying, drunk moment, Tess wonders if Jana is inviting her to sleep with her. Then she admonishes herself in her own room, which doesn't feel like her own. Her head is buzzing from driving all day. When she lies down, her limbs feel twitchy. Not enough movement and an excess of stress. She feels caught in a liminal space between exhaustion and nervousness—she is yawning but her heart is racing. Last night she was at her father's house, and now she's here. Her life is utterly transformed.

The external parts anyway.

Before they'd met, she'd seen Cam on Sundays, holding the arm of an older woman at a coffee shop. An ancient woman. A woman who dressed all in black, who wore a lace shawl, curled her hair and wore round glasses and thick stockings. Tess could practically smell the incense from the Orthodox church on her clothing. He accompanied the woman to her chair and helped her to sit. At first, Tess looked for similarities in their features, their gait, their posture—tendencies passed down through genetics—but saw none. The way he fluffed the pillows and turned away to get her coffee, missing her grateful smile, seemed to indicate that he requested nothing in return.

So why did he do it? He helped the woman into the café after church and ordered her a coffee whenever she needed one, and it wasn't his job. Probably was still doing it, amongst hundreds of other beautiful acts of dutiful love.

The cottage-cheese ceiling and the naked bulb hanging in the middle of the room seem like stage props in another person's life. A feeling like she's been here before. Lying quietly, she can hear her heart, a low drum at the base of her ribs. The streetlights coming in through the thin curtains illuminate a spider web in the corner. She considers the unfamiliar weight of the comforter on her chest and shoulders. Muffled reggae music upstairs, a drunken call from the street, a woman's laughter climbing the apartment stairwell. She wonders if people are drawn to cities because there's safety in human numbers. But is there really? People are unpredictable. People have to assume they'll be fine. Fate becomes probability, and comfort is found in statistics rather than in faith. She breathes in and out, counting. She feels the strange city air make its way through to her skin. Thick and humid.

She wants someone to touch her.

It is so bright in her room. Not from moonlight, but from millions of people lying awake, their eyes reflected in permanent spotlights. All the city a stage. The sheets hold a faint, stale smell of detergent, cigarettes, and dust. The apartment looked so clean. Tess can only assume that the spirit of the city snuck through the window into the bed to nestle in with her.

Chapter 3

It was at a party, the first time she'd spoken to him. Cam was behind the counter handing out drinks. He'd volunteered to do it, of course. She wasn't immediately drawn to him. He seemed like a regular guy. Kind. She didn't appreciate kindness yet.

As Tess asked for a beer, an older woman approached with searching eyes. She stepped behind the counter and reached out her arms.

"You could stop traffic with this face," the woman said, stepping close enough to press her breasts against Cam's chest. He took it in stride, gently easing the woman's arms off his body as he offered her a glass of water and a chair.

He had a British accent, and was a social worker. Tess wondered if he'd struggled with enough of his own demons to want to help others with theirs. Perhaps he was not afraid.

Not afraid of the sick and the ugly. Or of emptiness. Or of losing control.

He confronted all of the above, even though he must have known, as they all knew, that the caring professions could render a person as brittle as ice.

But he was energetic and kind, and had time for everyone. He had looked at her that day with what seemed to be genuine interest in what she wanted to drink.

Tess remembers envy at that party. A woman had begun dancing in the middle of the room, alone, and everyone watched her. She wore a sundress and her curly black hair trailed down to her waist. She smiled and urged others to dance. A feeling came over the room; it felt wrong to stand still, somehow, and let her dance alone. Yet the hesitation on the part of everyone in the room, Tess thought, was due to a collective understanding that no one would match her in confidence or beauty. Still, others wanted to feel as free as she looked. They were drawn in. Even Tess swayed to the music, wanting to prove that she, also, could be confident. Wanting to show, through her movements, that she had her own internal world as well, and it was a wonderful place, and she would not be inviting anyone in.

Cam later took a job as a social worker at a rehab center, and Tess took a job as a dental assistant. Though she'd finished her social work degree, she couldn't fathom being a social worker; she couldn't imagine telling someone how to live their life. She felt physically ill at the thought of children being hurt. She wouldn't work with older people, because loneliness broke her heart. She could never work with people with addiction—she couldn't summon the nerve. She would blame herself if her clients were unable to recover.

It felt presumptuous to assume that she could help anyone, yet it felt imperative that she try.

She stopped swaying at the party when she noticed Cam approaching the beautiful, dancing woman with a Guinness in his hand. He reached out his arm, but did not hand her the beer. He stepped around her, and gave it to the custodian who was on his way out after completing his shift. On his way back to the table, he asked Tess if she was having fun.

Then they stood around together and got drunk. He danced a little—badly, but with the grace and humour of a person who knows they should just sit down. They ate together and had more beer, and decided to meet up again to watch a movie.

He never made a move, so she assumed he was only interested in friendship.

Still, he always let her choose the movie.

When Tess realized what Cam was trying to tell her, it was already too late.

But the excitement filled her up. In retrospect, she thought about how his gaze lingered on her face even after she'd finished speaking. She observed the pride he took in introducing her to his family. She remembered the hurt in his eyes when she'd mentioned the hot new dentist.

Suddenly, he was attractive. How had she not noticed! She wanted to knit him warm woollen sweaters to outline his broad shoulders. His curls covered his beautiful eyes and she wanted to give him goosebumps as she brushed them away. His jaw pulsed as he chewed the roast chicken she wished she had been the one to cook for him.

Changes occurred within her. She thought about what to wear when meeting up with him. She lingered on his words, turned them around, dissected them. She wanted his words for herself. The room changed when he entered it. Energy shifted and feelings took shape and were coiled there between them like a taut rope. In dreams she was aroused by him, carrying that feeling through to the next day, wishing for time to speed up so she could see him again. She walked taller, she spoke louder. Cam loved her.

But he had given up before she could let him know that she felt the same way.

He had started dating Rita.

He and Rita were suddenly engaged.

That's when she decided to leave.

When she left home, during that long ten hour drive into the city, she observed her arm resting on the steering wheel. She had agreed to the tattoo with Cam when they were still just friends. They'd thought it would be fun to do it together. He got an eagle; she wanted a lobster.

"You might regret that," he'd said.

"I love lobsters," she'd said.

"Don't you want a smarter animal? An owl? They're clever, like you." He'd smiled then and she'd gone along with it.

Later she wished she'd followed her instinct. She felt more like a bottom feeder than the bird of wisdom.

Her phone rang.

She wanted to ignore the call, but wasn't there enough distance now? She didn't need to roll up the windows or even turn off the radio to hear him. His voice was perfect for telling stories, for directing people, for inspiring confidence. Deep and rich.

"I passed by your apartment earlier, and they said you'd left. For good?"

"Yep. I'm driving," she said.

Cam exhaled into the phone, an ocean sound, a shell to her ear.

"To go where?"

"A real city."

"Which one?"

"The one."

"Is this about your mum? Why didn't you tell me?" he asked.

"I didn't tell anyone."

That wasn't entirely true, but they were beyond telling one another the truth. She pictured his face: thick eyelashes lowered over his dark, deep-set eyes; his slightly crooked nose; his habit of tapping his fingers absentmindedly.

Tess wouldn't have put Cam and Rita together, but once they were an item she could see how they made sense. Rita was smart, funny, and organized. Tess admired her large Lebanese family and the way they argued with so much heart. It was almost unbearable to watch. She wanted that honesty in her life.

Rita kept Cam in line, and he encouraged her to be creative. He was attentive, kind to her friends and family, and when he thought no one was looking, he would nudge his face into her curls and whisper. Rita would burst out laughing, pushing him away only to draw him back in. They were lovely.

Tess had only let him know of her feelings for him once he was already dating Rita. She put him in an impossible position.

"How can you just leave? What about everything we've been through?" he asked.

The stars had been black the night of her birthday party, the night she'd finally slept with Cam—or maybe the moon was full, but either way he'd been looking at her when he should have been looking at the sky or his fiancée.

She moved around Astrid's small living room, her bikini bottom wet from their earlier dips in the ocean after Astrid convinced her to go in the water, flitting from conversation to conversation, obvious in her avoidance of him but with a clear vision of what was going to happen. The word *inevitable* bounced around her head.

She could feel he wanted her, and that had made her hot. Sexy. She had danced with Astrid right in front of Cam, shaking her hips and arching her back. She never would have done that if it hadn't been for the alcohol.

What had first been an ego boost became tantalizing, then an addiction. She hated this about herself; every time she loved and desired someone she gave all. She wanted to possess him. In the car she'd practice conversations with him, in the shower she'd observe her body as though from his perspective, in her bed she'd cry guilty, delicious tears.

She'd never really stolen before.

She'd shoplifted a few times as a kid—grabbing some candy from the open bins in the discount bulk stores but, in her defence, she'd thought they were testers. Once her mother caught her and told her to stop, but she didn't. She and Astrid would bike down to the strip malls on warm summer days and casually fill their pockets without anyone noticing. They were quiet kids from hard-working families and no one would have suspected. The adrenaline of those moments saved her from a simmering boredom.

When she started sneaking around with Cam even though he was engaged to Rita, she felt her life to be full and exciting, and she felt the weight of his words—the ones whispered into her ear late at night, hands on her hips and lips on her neck. Words coming from the secret place where desire takes root. How he'd always loved her. How she meant the world to him.

In the car, she willed herself to stay strong and to focus on her goal of escape. It was a matter of pride.

"Cam, what have we been through? I've been dragged through a lie and you needed an accomplice."

She wished she'd been prepared for this call. She hadn't expected it. Sweat sat on her upper lip, poured out of the backs of her legs, tickled her scalp. She shouldn't have answered.

"It wasn't a lie. You know how I felt about you."

He was already losing patience, but she didn't care.

"How did you feel about Rita?"

"That's beside the point, Tess."

"How is it beside the point?" she said, wondering how many times they would replay this conversation. "You hurt us both because you want people to love you."

"Rita understands now. She does."

"I doubt that. I didn't need you to open me up, I didn't need you to save me," she said, as her throat closed in on itself like a fist. "I don't need your pity."

She hung up and threw her phone on the seat next to her. She had to slow her breath. She knew Cam cared about her. He had helped her through difficult patches in her life. He'd been a good friend. Always there with a warm shoulder and a cold beer. Then a few more. She was being unfair by making herself the victim.

All those years she could have had him, and was too blind to see it.

She didn't need anyone.

Traffic was thick and she had to focus on driving. She was entering the system of passages and arteries that led into the heart of the city. Someone cut her off and a man gave her the finger. She tried to speed up but, at that moment, the skyline appeared in the distance: an electric blue cross on a hill, the teetering skyscrapers of downtown. Her bright island oasis.

The half-moon of summer winked through the purple shades of dusk rolling across the sky. She felt like an idiot.

A few days later, Tess is tired from the stimulation. She feigns interest but all she wants is for the city to let her sleep. Her dreams are more vivid than reality. Her mother visits when she can—more a feeling than an actual vision—a shudder in her body. She wakes again and again to loss. She wonders why the dreams feel so real after leaving home. She wonders why her dreaming mind can't remember that her mother is gone. It is as though upon closing her eyes she travels through time and space, tearing through to another dimension, her memory wrinkled and folded as her wicked mind plays tricks.

"Tess, are you all right?" Jana asks, repeatedly.

"I'm adapting," Tess responds, cringing at the falsehood.

She hopes Jana doesn't think she's shirking her responsibility to find a job.

She finally contacts Meals on Wheels and decides that's a good start.

Chapter 4

Tess rides Jana's bike through the city, searching for the address to which she'll deliver a warm meal for a senior. She's never delivered food before. She just started volunteering at La Popote roulante, as Meals on Wheels is known, and she spent the last two weeks sitting in a sunny office that smells like curry, learning how to keep track of the volunteer schedule while making sure the kitchen staff and bicycle delivery persons have their instructions.

No peas for this delivery. Also remember the doorbell is broken.

She'd already made a note for Olivier, but he called in sick. Could she drop it off on her way home? He speaks to her in French most of the time, and doesn't seem to mind when she answers in English. Does he know she would speak French, if it weren't for her pride? She doesn't like making mistakes. Besides, he's one of the most beautiful men she's ever met, which makes her wary. He must know he's beautiful. Beautiful men are the luckiest people on earth, and they can't possibly be beautiful and good.

The apartment is number 124, a squat, square building in the shadow of the Jewish General Hospital. The area around it is gently sloping from the hill at the heart of the city. The neighbourhood bustles with colourful sari shops and steamy Vietnamese restaurants. Tess feels the energy of the neighbourhood, feels solidarity with people searching out a new life.

Then her mind challenges her emotions—what if these sari shops and restaurants have been here for decades? She shouldn't assume they're new. And what right does she have to compare her low-stakes decisions to people who have put their lives on the line to travel halfway around the world?

She parks these paralyzing thoughts and thinks about the task at hand. Then, chastising herself for putting off thoughts of privilege, she locks her bike to the post. She is happy to be in a place that is big enough she can feel passionate and get involved, yet stay at arm's length. Cam used to say it must be exhausting to be her, with her whirring mind that never stops tripping over guilt.

She gathers the package containing the meal—baked chicken, carrots, potatoes, applesauce, and muffin—like the offering that it is. A smell of hospital food wafts through the air, reminding her of chicken noodle soup in a paper cup. Reminding her of the time her soup went cold, on the desk in the hospice, as her mother died.

Her shadow follows her reluctantly up the steps like an accordion. She opens the front door and looks for the apartment number on the greasy screen. She rings his apartment.

The client doesn't answer through the speaker, but presses the buzzer for what seems like forever. The building smells like the inside of a microwave. She finds door 5A, knocks, and waits. No one answers. She tries again, double-checking the address.

Apart from the moments where she thinks about Cam or her mother, or when her mind turns in circles, she's beginning to feel somewhat moored. Grounded, even. She sticks to a schedule. She washes dishes, and cooks when she can. She even lugs the garbage, recycling, and compost down three flights of stairs on the appointed days. At a garage sale, she found a cheap mirror and some other items to make her room feel cozier: a picture frame, a poster, a small rug. She hopes these will make her room feel like someone else's room. Someone who belongs.

She only drinks at night.

She thought she would miss the clear night sky of home, the trees along the coast, and the ebb of the ocean. That a city in constant, unpredictable motion could have a positive effect on her is a surprise. She finds herself moving more slowly than she needs to, enjoying the grit on her skin, in her teeth, the faint lingering lacing of dust. Particles of people. All of whom have chosen to let parts of their histories unfold here.

Tess receives a message from Olivier on her phone: *If you're going to Hewitt's house, watch out! He's a grump. Just go straight in, he'll be there.*

She was surprised when she met Olivier at the Meals on Wheels office, and even more surprised that he would be her supervisor. He seemed too young and attractive to work there. He seemed confident and cunning, rather than compassionate and caring. She's probably prejudiced against beautiful people, but she can accept that most of her interpretations are probably her own deep, hidden desires projected onto the screen of her mind.

She tries the door and opens it ever so slightly.

"*Bonjour*? Hello? It's Meals on Wheels, *La Popote roulante*."

No answer.

She stands at the threshold of the apartment, a tingling in her body. It takes a moment for her eyes to adjust to the darkness. How could Olivier not have mentioned this? She pulls her hair away from her face. Floor to ceiling, the apartment lists under the weight of soiled objects that appear to have been picked up on the street. Cardboard boxes, empty cans of tomato paste, glass jars, bottles of Tylenol, flyers, and phone books. All in a jumble of stacks around the room. Every conceivable space is filled.

Incredulous, she takes a step forward. A Scottish family crest is nailed to the wall just next to the front door. The cracked tile is painted with a red and white shield with yellow tassels on the sides and three owls looking just beyond her right shoulder.

A name on the crest: Hewitt.

An old baby stroller propped up on top of an ironing board like an absurd altar. A shower curtain on the floor. Patches of yellow wall like rays of sun through a dark canopy of trees. Then, she spots him shuffling slowly around the corner, probably to avoid knocking over the piles of boxes. He steps gingerly, like a deer. He holds a delicate teacup. He's a slight man, balding, and he wears a beige knitted sweater and slacks.

Tess takes a step back towards the door and knocks again. "*Bonjour,* hello, Mr. Hewitt?"

What language did he speak? She hopes English will be fine, and guesses it will be, especially in this neighbourhood, especially with a name like Hewitt. He looks in her direction, his eyes large and limpid. It seems to take him a moment to register that there is a woman standing at his door. His brow furrows.

"Who are you? Where's the regular guy?" he asks, his voice splintered and rough.

"He wasn't feeling well, so they asked me to fill in," she answers.

He seems to acknowledge her by turning his mouth down at the sides, though he says nothing, continuing to shuffle through the detritus in his apartment.

"Where should I put the food?" Tess asks. She takes a few steps, trying not to brush against anything while she looks for spaces to land her feet.

She holds up the package, the warmth of it seeping through the bottom of the bag. She is supposed to chat and make sure the client isn't too lonely. She's supposed to make sure he has everything he needs, but she'll put the food down and leave. Any effort at friendliness will likely amplify his loneliness. Besides, this man obviously isn't in the mood for companionship. He's stuck between a bedside table and a torn olive-green couch. He points in the direction of the bedside table.

"Do you have cutlery?" she asks.

"Somewhere, I'm sure. No peas, I hope," he says.

She double-checks her paper.

"No peas," she confirms.

"Just leave it there on the table."

She wonders how she'll get to the table when she hears her phone ding. She checks, in case it's Olivier.

I forgot to say he is blind.

Tess sets down the food, and stands amongst his things. She's not sure whether to leave. She looks at him with fresh eyes. It doesn't seem like a safe space for a person with blindness to live but, then again, what does she know? The old man takes care of his body and appearance—his hair is parted and brushed, his clothes tidy and clean.

He doesn't match his surroundings. He looks like a man who would frequent a library or university. He seems made for an environment of polished stone, dark wood, and hushed tones. He should be walking through landscapes of murky green light and low grey skies. He should be in a study with wing chairs and pocket watches, globes and maps, ships in bottles, fossils, shells, and driftwood. He looks urban in an old-world kind of way.

He does not fit in with the vast emptiness of his accumulated junk.

Could the random objects in the apartment be comforting? Maybe a sense of self is contained in one's possessions—memories roused by objects.

Tess knows that sifting through a person's possessions is like piecing together a puzzle that will never be complete. She thinks of the objects she'd collected when her mother died—her mother's nightgowns, glasses, recipes, and tweezers. Astrid had helped her clean out her mother's things, and had laughed when Tess insisted on keeping her mother's tweezers. The truth is, looking at them conjured her mother, sitting on her bed in her nightgown, legs crossed, eyebrows raised, tweezers in hand.

"You'll have to pluck my eyebrows when I'm too old to do it myself," she'd say.

It saddened Tess that her mother thought she'd live to be old.

Or maybe this man had actually decided not to surround himself with memories, but to block them out. Maybe this was junk, and he wanted to keep himself barricaded inside a prison bereft of meaning.

But why?

If this was just random crap, or if he didn't understand the health risk the boxes posed—fire hazard being the main one— then maybe she should ask some probing questions. Though she wasn't working as a social worker, she had the degree, and goodness knows she'd been trained to ask pertinent, leading questions.

"Do you believe in your dreams?" He asks a question first.

"Sorry?" she says.

"Do you believe dreams show you the truth?"

He is leaning against the side of the olive green couch, his chin raised and his eyes searching. His body is completely still as he speaks, only his fingers twitch slightly, as though conducting the rhythm of his thoughts. She notices that he has an accent unfamiliar to her—perhaps different accents blended together—hard consonants softened by dipping vowels.

Tess is unsure how to answer.

"Someone once told me a dream is a body's most honest communication with itself. Do you believe that?" Mr. Hewitt seems annoyed now.

"For what it's worth, I take note of my dreams," she says.

Tess is not being fully honest. She'd relied on dreams to help her wade through grief. After her mother's death, the few blessed nights she capsized into a proper sleep, she dreamed her mother was alive. The balm of her mind's deception was worth it, even as she woke, slowly, to the cruel shock that she would never see her mother again. The dreams had eased the painful transition to emotional homelessness.

"Do you remember your dreams days or weeks after you've had them?" he asks.

Why the obsession with dreams? Despite herself, she answers him. He is disarming and endearing, like a child who immediately takes a strange adult into their confidence.

"I suppose I remember them when I wake up, and sometimes a feeling will stay with me throughout the day," she says. "But I don't remember them for any length of time."

"Do you know that dreams help cement your memories from the day? Dreaming about an event helps to create a long-term memory. If you recall an event while awake, then you alter the memory. Why do you think we remember most events in our lives, but not our dreams?"

"I—I don't know. Maybe because dreams are not real life," she answers.

"How do you know real life is not a dream? A dream is witness to our deepest desires and fears. Dreams tell us about ourselves. What did you say your name was, again?" he asks, looking beyond her head.

"I don't think I said, but it's Tess."

"Right. Tess of the D'Urbervilles. I had a dream about you," he says. He hunches over a little, his shoulders against his ears.

"Sorry?"

"Are you?"

"Am I what?" Tess is confused.

"Are you sorry?"

"Uh, I am sorry, because I'm having trouble following ..."

"Do you like to read?"

He smiles now, his teeth crooked and surprisingly white. He walks slowly to a corner where he pulls a book out of a sagging box, a deliberation in his movements bordering on reverence. How strange, Tess thinks, to treat a book like a delicate object yet have an apartment in such a state of disarray.

Mr. Hewitt holds the book out in her direction, open to a page, and asks her to read any paragraph she chooses. May as well. This may be the only entertainment she'll have all day. She takes the book. It feels damp.

"The sea is everything. It covers seven tenths of the terrestrial globe. Its breath is pure and healthy." She looks up and Mr. Hewitt is smiling, so she continues. "It is an immense desert, where man is never lonely, for he feels life stirring on all sides. The sea is only the embodiment of a supernatural and wonderful existence ... It is nothing but love and emotion."

"Do you like to read?" he asks again.

"Oh, yeah."

"Calvino, the writer, you know, Italo Calvino, said in one of his books, I can't remember which one, and I'm paraphrasing here, what makes reading resemble lovemaking is that within both of them times and spaces open."

"Oh?" Tess says. She thinks she should leave.

"Maybe that thought had occurred to you too. Where are you from?" he asks.

"I'm from the East Coast," she says.

"Ah yes, we have a longitudinal connection. I can tell you're just passing through. You won't drop anchor here. You know, we're all travellers, searching for happiness."

His eyes are so sad, Tess's heart pulls a little. She takes a step closer to him, wondering if he can hear her or smell her, if he has heightened senses with the loss of his sight. She wonders when he lost his sight. How he lost it.

"What does happiness look like for you?" she asks, looking at the laugh lines running from his eyes down his cheeks.

"It doesn't look like much. I see darkness most of the time," he says.

"Oh, I'm so sorry." She winces at her cruelty. "Of course." She wants to leave.

"It's all right. I can still perceive what's important. It helps not to look at something directly, but to see beyond it, in fact."

He walks around the edge of the couch, kicks a plastic bag out of the way, and sits down.

"You know humans navigate with vision and memory. I'm working on using auditory navigation. In other words, training myself to be like a bird. Did you know true navigation is the ability to reach a destination without landmarks? Imagine we could sense the earth's magnetic field. We have such terrible awareness of our environment."

"Yes, I suppose that's true."

"So, I'm in training. I'm never bored."

"Well, you're set then," Tess says, trying to sound bright.

"Ha! Imagine." He shakes his head. "Are you daft? I'm joking. I have nothing to do here. I never leave this place. I'm reduced to this. I'm denied any multidimensionality. The other guy at least reads to me."

"Oh, sorry."

Tess arranges her features into what she would consider an expression of kindness and understanding, despite the fact that he can't see it.

She stammers as Mr. Hewitt stands up, shaking his head. It seems he's seen through her and she's not worth it. He's walking away from her, towards the kitchen. She'd met gruff old men like him before, cranky yet elegant, and she'd been annoyed at her readiness to conform to whatever they'd wanted her to be. Men who ran the world—the perpetually disappointed father, teacher, name-your-authority-figure. The ones who'd set the rules for so long.

And yet. How could he be an authority figure, he who lives here?

"You need to stop saying sorry!" he shouts, from the next room.

"Oh, right. Sorry!" she shouts back. To her relief he chuckles.

Tess takes an opportunity to look around some more. The apartment is a fair size, and probably could have been quite nice, but there's nothing to suggest that an actual person lives here. It feels like a messy warehouse. A cardboard box to her left contains jumbles of old cell phones, keyboards and wires, newspapers, calendars and books. Torn slips of paper. The smell of dust and cobwebs. Objects aged in shadows and webs, rather than in time.

Mr. Hewitt hasn't returned, so she picks up a newspaper written in Spanish. The pages are taken from the sports section, *deportes*, with photos of soccer players sporting long hair and tiny shorts exposing muscular, smooth thighs. Tess wonders if it is possible to decipher a person's life from their piles of junk—an expression of self-preservation, perhaps.

Then she spots a book: maroon leather cover, soft from use, with a black binding. She opens the crisp pages to small, slanted handwriting like tendrils sloping up a garden fence, some words in English, most in Spanish. She brings the pages closer to her face and breathes in.

Tess knows she's holding some kind of journal stuffed full of private letters. Thick and heavy. She knows it shouldn't be left in a box. On an impulse, and without thinking much about it, she slips the book into her purse.

La primera parte - la primavera

I'm not sure why I write this. Perhaps I want a record of these days and feelings so when I'm older I can pity my naïveté. Or envy my hope.

The café was located in a new *barrio* and it overlooked the river's edge. It was perfect. We tossed our backpacks on a patio table, which was enclosed in a protective border of jacaranda trees. It smelled like spring; the air like a caress. I was aroused. We never use the same café twice. A waiter in a white shirt stuck his head out to acknowledge us, but didn't come to take our order. We waited.

Bárbara asked me if I'd read Nietzsche. I considered lying. I've had enough opportunities to read him, but those days I was not able to follow the logic of abstract thought or concentrate on intricate ideas. I was so distracted by my physical body. Prickles of sweat under my arms, my erection hiding in my pants, and other shameful, yet life-affirming reactions to her presence.

She pulled her books, newspapers, and leaflets out of a bag, arranged them in piles and set them at right angles. I watched as she organized her materials and flyers: *The Rise of the Working Class*, *Balancing Production and Consumption,* and *Social Justice Begins with You!* I worried she was being careless. Too obvious. Maybe she's having an effect on me after all.

Funny to think about how people affect us or change the course of events. Our friends and lovers etch their initials in our hearts and those become the maps of our lives.

I felt warm in the shade, and a bit nauseous.

My grandmother says it's my nerves. She's always making me broth for my stomach. When I looked up, the sky appeared like cerulean puzzle pieces through the violet trees.

I said this out loud, something about the leaves and their contrast to the sky, and she shook her head. She smiled. Everyone else found my way of speaking pretentious, but Bárbara didn't mind. She found me sentimental and foolish but she liked it. She said those who fashion themselves as poets can be successful. Those deft with words can become conduits or mouthpieces. They can even be appointed as diplomats and ambassadors.

Words can persuade, capture, and ensnare. Or incriminate.

Eventually, the waiter appeared at our table and we rushed to put away our pamphlets. He had a yellow stain on his white shirt. He introduced himself as though we'd be spending days in his café, but he never looked us in the eye. We ordered two Americanos. He said his name was Francisco.

Bárbara and my grandmother were the only two people in the world to read my poems. Bárbara kept my poems crumpled in her pockets. She's a natural leader with ideals. She believes non-traditional education to be the antidote to ignorance, which she thinks is the cause of fascism and tyranny. She thinks the people just need a voice. *El pueblo unido jamás será vencido.* She believes it can all be undone, and redone.

We aren't yet afraid of death, or of life.

When I think about it, her features, taken separately, are nothing special, but when considered together, they have the effect of a car crash. You can't look away.

"Nietzsche says there are no facts, only interpretations. You need to know they're going to blame us for anything that happens, and they'll twist the truth around to suit their story. They'll never accept that they drove us to it."

She took a sip of her coffee, and lit us each a cigarette. I liked how she turned her head when she did it. I liked how the grey taste of smoke blended with the bitter coffee. I didn't know who "they" were, but the way she looked at me lent me a sudden manly self-appraisal.

"I know the truth," I said. This was a measured disclosure on my part. I wanted to say what she wanted to hear. I'd decided whose side I was on.

At least, I thought I had.

"That's why I need you to do something for me," she said, handing me an itinerary along with my train ticket.

I indicated with my posture that I was listening, even though my head had started to spin. I needed to figure out what was going on. I needed to be smarter.

This story begins much earlier, during the last month of my last year of high school. I was confronted with the question of what I might wish to do with the rest of my life. Señor Vacas handed me the paper with an encouraging smile, confident I would know what to write. He even called me son, which he'd not done before and which, as far as I could remember, no man had ever done. My father died. I was raised by women.

My mother would love it if I studied dentistry or banking. She's practical. But as I sat at my desk, the clock ticking, the sound of pencils to paper, my mind flipping through a Rolodex of the usual professions, I couldn't imagine the eternity of a career: performing the same tasks—like looking at rotten teeth or calculating interest rates—for an entire lifetime.

I wanted to camouflage myself behind words. Bending time! Moving through a maze of ideas, and bringing other people with me! I wanted nothing more than to have the freedom to be a writer. I'd so far only managed to put together a not-too-compelling collection of facts and figures—more like a journal than anything else. I wanted to tell a good story, but all I had to guide me was my own life.

It's amazing that we have these tools, symbols and odd sounds to convey our deepest thoughts and our bitterest agonies; that we can transmit a portion of our own psyche into someone else's, even if just for a moment.

Isn't it?

I think words will likely just lead me back to myself.

But I wanted to go on the adventure. Anything to avoid my mother's boring life. Routine had become a crutch to help my mother through the days. I wonder whether routine keeps us away from something essential. I hoped she had a secret passion. She made eggs, sausages, and toast every morning because my dead English father liked them at breakfast. She needed to make his absence a presence in our lives. Then she'd make her lunch and leave for her job as an accountant for the transport corporation. She worked every day from eight to four.

At the last instant, in class, I wrote my answer to the question of what I would do with my life. I wrote: "purveyor of justice."

Martín reached over the desk and handed me a note. It occurred to me as I unfolded the paper that Martín, who is my best friend, wouldn't be expected to answer any question about his future, his father having more than enough means and influence to determine the course of his life. He left his future goals blank. Instead, on the other side of the page, he'd drawn Señor Vacas (it was unmistakable, for his back which bends like a cane) with the addition of a big hairy erection. In the picture, Vacas was standing in front of Señorita Alarcón, the history teacher, with her tight bun, beige skirts, and thick calves. He'd drawn hearts for eyes and a bubble coming out of his mouth with the word *ardeo*.

I burn.

This was appropriate; he was our Latin teacher.

I felt an obligation to reciprocate. When Señor Vacas turned his attention to another student, I tore a fresh piece of paper from my notebook and drew a picture of Señorita Alarcón lying on a desk with her legs spread and hearts in her eyes, a bubble coming out of her mouth and the word *arsum*.

We're burning.

When Martín saw it, he stifled a laugh, gave me a thumbs up and folded the paper into an airplane. We often acted younger than we were. I think we wanted to hide our hopes which were too frightening to name. I followed the arc of the flying sheet, which glided across the room to land at the feet of Bárbara Bianchi.

I found my grandmother pretending to wipe down the counters. She was rearranging all the dishes my mother had already put away. She wore her favourite dark orange shirt, which was tight across her broad bosom and flared out like a tiny dress. She never wears a bra, she believes they cause cancer, so I could see the outline of her nipples through the fabric. Her large earrings dangled around her face, and her blue eyeshadow smudged along her forehead. She used to be gorgeous. She was known as "Liria the beautiful," and she sang like Mercedes Sosa.

It was Friday afternoon and we had an ice cream date. Most people hung out with their grandparents out of a sense of obligation, but I loved hanging out with my *abuelita*. We sat at the small, damp, wooden tables, and she told me about how she used to clean rich women's houses while their husbands would find ways to hang around at home, watching her and begging her to go to their beds.

She sleeps with glasses so she can understand clearly the meaning of her dreams. She says she has no need for a man. She planted sunflowers last year and one grew so large, she treated it like a lover. It was awkward to see her outside, talking to the enormous flower as she bustled around the garden, stopping from time to time to caress it. The sunflower leaned its enormous black face and yellow head towards her, its petals open and ready for an embrace.

I told her about the question they'd asked at school, about our plans for the future.

Sure enough, she said I shouldn't be blamed for not knowing my future. They should be ashamed for asking. Even the best laid plans go to shit through no fault of one's own. She said those *huevones* ask stupid questions, and should instead tell us what they think we should do, so we can go ahead and do the opposite. She said no one knows what they want or who they are until they're at least forty, and then they spend the rest of their lives lamenting the fact that they'll likely never get there.

She's the real deal.

I thought that I would never love anyone as much as I loved my grandmother. I thought that until the day Bárbara Bianchi spoke directly to me. A birth and a death in one breath. It happened after I'd been called to the head office at school with Martín. You'll forgive me for jumping around my memories—they're not linear and neither is time. We arrived to find Bárbara standing next to the principal's mahogany desk, an inscrutable look on her determined face. I hadn't seen it before, but now I did. She was a candle, her face glowing in the light of my admiration. She was perfection in an imperfect world.

I froze, assuming that she had found and shared our lewd drawings (the paper airplane!) and I'd been sheltered enough to be frightened of my teachers, my mother, and the prospect of suspension. I was even more terrified of girls. I'd had some experience, sure, but Bárbara's determined energy unnerved me. The teachers paid us no mind; they were discussing the recent election. Martín and I had no idea what we were doing there. Then they told us in a few words, barely turning their attention to us, that we would volunteer with a student youth group for the next few weeks.

It didn't seem like volunteering if they were obliging us to do it. Martín complained. He said we had to study, he said we didn't have enough time. I knew he was worried about letting down his soccer team. We hadn't accepted that we could be involved in our education beyond a resigned understanding that we had no choice, and we'd thought even less about our communities, religion, or politics. Our own choices, and the influence those might have on the trajectories of our lives, or millions of other lives, eluded us.

Bárbara shot me a look as if asking whether I agreed with my friend. I saw an image that still haunts me now: Martín and Bárbara, twin images of a mountain in a lake. The girl with eyes like wet stones who possessed such a clear sense of herself, and the boy whose house I'd gotten to know like my own, whose thoughts were my thoughts and whose pain was my pain. They were staring at one another.

Then the teachers asked me a question. I said something I thought they'd like to hear. I was good at that. The skill might save my life.

I stood behind Bárbara in line, trying not to get too close. When she pulled her hair into a ponytail, a butterfly emerged from her hand and fluttered to the floor. I picked it up and tapped her on the shoulder.

"Your *papelito*."

She turned and looked at me. Then she spoke, her voice softer than expected given her hard gaze.

"It's not a drawing."

I almost died, thinking of our crass drawings of the teachers.

"It's a brochure for a movie. A bunch of us are going just before Mariana's party. Maybe you can make it?"

I had trouble finding my voice, but Martín cut in. Of course he did.

"Sure, we can make it. We'll be there."

She turned to go, and I saw her white socks on her smooth legs, walking away. That moment drew a line. I had lost control. I would never be the same.

After school I met Esteban at his uncle Silvio's café. He gives us free espressos and biscuits and always lights our cigarettes, so long as we don't annoy the customers.

We sat on the patio, watching people going by. We marked on a napkin how many attractive girls walked past. We'd reached eleven when Martín arrived. He said he was late because he'd been with his maid, Cecilia. He made us smell his fingers—said he hadn't washed them. It's true, they smelled like he hadn't washed for a while, but they also smelled like lemon and iron. Not at all the way I imagine Cecilia would smell. Cecilia with the braids and sweet face. Cecilia with the freckles and frocks. I don't think either of us knew what to say, so we just smiled, and continued counting girls. But I don't think our hearts were in it after that.

We missed the movie, but Martín, Esteban, and I found Mariana's neighbourhood and picked up wine and cigarettes. We passed a tall grey wall, and I asked them how they'd decorate it if they could do graffiti (we decided we would, one day soon). Bárbara and her friends appeared then. Her boots were heavy on the concrete, hands deep in her pockets. Under the street lamp, her dark hair took on a reddish hue. I didn't say it, but I thought I'd paint the wall in different shades of black and grey, with the silhouette of a woman in yellow and red.

She didn't say much, but led us through the neighbourhood until we arrived at Mariana's yellow house, half-engulfed by the shrubbery out front. Mariana was outside smoking with a couple of girls, and she waved when she saw us and brought us around the side of the house to the back.

I recognized a bunch of people from school standing in the back garden, where some meat was smoking on the grill. Mariana had strung up streamers and lights from the trees. The doors into the house were open, and inside was a wood-paneled room with a table of empanadas, sausages and vegetables, dips and salsa, and ashtrays. Bottles of Coca-Cola, Fanta, and wine sat on another table pushed against the wall. Two large maps hung on the wooden walls: one of our country, one of the world.

The chairs were already taken so Martín, Esteban, Bárbara and I stood around. Martín drank his glass of wine in one gulp, lit a cigarette, and got more wine.

"Have any of you ever been anywhere else?"

We stood there looking at one another.

"I mean, have any of you ever been anywhere other than that fucking dot?" Bárbara pointed at the map of our country, our city, and her long hair slipped across her shoulder and fell down her back like a sheet of honey-coloured satin.

"That dot, I'll have you know, houses the best literature, architecture, music and soccer players on this fucking continent," Martín said, coming back with two cups of wine (one for me).

I hadn't seen him this worked up about an abstraction before. He was usually pretty easygoing, even if he had a tendency to be grumpy when his team lost or when he was hungry.

"Hey, do you want an empanada? I'm grabbing one," I said.

He shook his head as he listened to Bárbara argue that the conditions of its people provided a true measure of a country's worth.

"The rest of the country doesn't contribute anything. They're just stupid peasants."

Bárbara took a step back, furious. Ready to throw her wine in his face. Mariana came then and told us to go outside. A band had shown up and we had to listen and dance.

I tried to figure out why Martín had been so hostile to Bárbara—as far as I knew he was just trying to get into Mariana's pants. But it seemed to me, as the night went on, that Bárbara might have been talking to me, and only me, to get back at him, and that was making him angry. He became louder and more belligerent, and I was reduced to a puddle under her attention. She told me of her plans to work with poor people, but her eyes shone with watery reflections and she stood so close.

She was more driven than anyone I'd ever met. She reminded me of my mother in the way she was organized and liked to make plans, but she was different from my mother in that her plans had purpose. The wine lightened my brain and darkened the edges, and I said I would join her. I meant that I'd join her wherever she wanted me to go, but she understood me in a more immediate sense, and told me to meet her the next day.

In the morning, I took an Aspirin for my headache and drank my grandmother's cricket piss (her version of coffee) and thought about the previous night. Though not much had happened, I sensed that my life was different.

Maybe my mother sensed it too. That morning, she made me toast and asked me not to hang out with people involved in politics. I told her I'd have to live in a cave.

Bárbara showed up when she said she would. She wore a navy-blue sweater and jeans and carried her huge suede bag. I couldn't believe I was alone with her and that I'd get to spend the day with her! In my head, I thanked Martín for being an asshole. The week before, Bárbara and I hadn't even exchanged two words.

She seemed to study my eyes, my hair, my hands, as though looking for details.

Even though I felt I knew her, I also understood that she didn't know me, yet. Martín and I had always been best friends and we even looked alike (some people thought we were twins), but I wanted to differentiate myself as quickly as I could.

"I hope you weren't upset by what Martín said."

"It's not your fault," she said, smiling. "To think I used to like him."

Energy blew through me and out of me, leaving me like a deflated balloon. She had liked him, and that's why he stirred up such intense feelings. He probably liked her too, but had pretended to like Mariana because she was better-looking. Superficial bastard. I decided I'd no longer be considered identical to Martín. I'd had enough of being his shadow.

Other people lined up for the bus behind us, turning their faces towards the sunlight filtered through the glass of the bus stop. I wanted them all to know that she used to like him, and now liked me. I wanted them to see me with her.

She was still looking at me, so I asked if she did a lot of volunteer work, or something.

It took her some time to answer. She swung her bag around so it lay across her stomach like a baby in her arms, while she dug inside it for cigarettes. She said her parents had made her help out in an orphanage. The cigarette lay between her lips. She lit it by tilting her head slightly to the side.

"That's cool," I said, rather stupidly.

"Yeah. Except I came from that orphanage."

She looked out at the street, narrowing her eyes as she inhaled. That explained her anger. Martín's idiotic assertions were a direct assault on her identity. I didn't yet know how to respond to someone else's pain when it was expressed so openly. What did any of this mean to her, how would I find out, and what would I say?

"Do you think I could have a cigarette too?" is all I managed. "I didn't know you were adopted."

"Neither did I. But I'm going to find my parents, no matter what I do. I just can't be distracted, and I can't be sidelined by people like Martín."

"Oh, he's harmless," I said, scuffing a shape in the dirt at my feet. "All bark and no bite."

The bus arrived, so we threw away our cigarettes. We sat together in silence on the bus, watching the city—the one we knew—slowly disintegrate through our window. It became poorer with every kilometer. Her arm rested against mine, occasionally pushing into it as she shifted her body in her seat. I kept my arm where it was. As we made our way further from the city center, the city became unrecognizable. Piles of garbage, mangy dogs. It was clear to me that the people here had no help—except for us? I only had a basic understanding of what we were going to do and felt entirely unprepared. Hungover and confused. Hungry and horny. She'd mentioned something about a restaurant.

"I'd like to go to the countryside someday," I said, trying to feel inspired.

"Good. We'll live in the country together then. It's settled."

We got off the bus and walked towards the expanse of makeshift shacks of the shantytowns: red, purple, yellow and brown, built with materials found around the city and precariously balanced atop one another. Tin roofs held up water barrels, lines of clothes dried in the sun. Wires grasped for the power grid—tentacles reaching out from the periphery. I had passed this place a few times in the car or on a bus, but never really looked at it.

Bárbara wore her black work boots and had stuffed her suede bag full of old clothes. I noticed there were no streetlights and made a mental note to leave before dark. We came to a white clinic with a sign written in large blue paint: Jesús Salva. A bustling market further down. Bárbara directed me to turn down a small side street and we entered the labyrinthine pathways of the slum.

PART II

NAVIGATION

Chapter 5

Olivier leans in to say goodbye, kissing her on one cheek, then the other. She turns her head the wrong way and hits him in the face with her long earring.

"I guess I should get going," she says.

Yet she remains rooted to the spot. She looks at his hands, his sun bleached nails, and wonders if he can feel the heat emanating from her body. They're standing outside the Meals on Wheels office after closing up together. They'd been chatting about silly things—how they each want a vegetable garden, how they'd love to go to India, and how they're afraid of small talk. Tess may have exaggerated the first two to speed up the intimacy with Olivier, but the last fear was real.

"You know what, if you're not busy, I could make you a cup of coffee? I actually live about a block from here," he says.

Tess smiles, not too much. Just enough. Her smile is not nearly as beautiful as his.

"It's my turn to get groceries." She turns her head and hesitates. "But I could use a coffee."

Olivier brings her to a wall, which is covered by a large mural of a woman's face. The layers of paint are lined in a way that suggests wrinkles. Next to the mural is a door, and Tess is surprised when he opens it and invites her in.

His apartment is a small room with three grey walls, one red brick wall, and a small bathroom. There is a closed door—the bedroom, or a closet perhaps.

A small Chilean restaurant next door sells empanadas. The soft, sweet smell of grease seeps into the room.

He closes the door. It is heavy. This action shifts Tess's giddiness over his attentions into an uneasy awareness that she's alone with a man she barely knows. She usually trusts her instincts; still, she's aware of stories that end with shaking heads and an assertion that someone had "asked for it."

She'd never felt unsafe with Cam.

"I like your place," she says.

She doesn't really. It's too empty, but she doesn't know what else to say in the face of his demure expectation. He offers her the choice of a chair—the only one he seems to own—or a woollen blanket that he has folded into a rectangle. Teresa chooses the blanket and sits cross-legged on the floor. She takes off her boots, remembering her mismatched socks, and decides he probably won't notice. He's dropped his backpack, which is covered in buttons: *Land Back. No Evictions.* He's preparing something on the other side of the room, at a small sink, and bangs dishes together.

"Ostie."

He's broken a dish. After sweeping it up, he brings over the coffee mugs and milk, stopping to grab a joint on top of his desk. He says he used to smoke too much, but now only when he has company. She feels mild disappointment; he probably invited her as an excuse to smoke. She leans back against the brick wall. The uneven, scratchy ridges serrate her spine. He takes a seat on a chair across from her, slouches, and places an ankle over his knee. She has to tilt her head to look up at him.

"So, Tess, you studied social work? What attracted you to that?"

He saw her resumé, of course. But is this still an interview?

She has to think. Had she been "attracted" to social work? He probably wants her to say she likes to help people.

"I don't know." She looks into her coffee. "If I'm a social worker, then I can advocate for people who are overlooked."

This sounds false. Even to her.

"I can also be sure I'm safely on the other side."

People pitied her because they knew her mother was unwell, even though no one spoke about it directly. Her proud mother hid herself away, but neighbours, teachers, and friends made it their business to know, and to let Tess know that they knew, through their concern and their questions. Their self-satisfied smiles let Tess know they'd done their best, and they wouldn't interfere. But they knew.

She used to write cards for her mother. Drawings of cats and balloons and hearts. Little messages to make her laugh. She imagined her mother might say that the card had "made her day." She didn't know why she wanted her to say those words, exactly, but the desire was too strong to ignore. Tess isn't sure when she gave up.

"Ah, but 'overlooked' is in the eye of the beholder," Olivier says. "Often those overlooked just want to be left alone."

She nods, thinking, still, of her mother. Difficult to be alone in a place where everyone knows everyone else's business. Where people only survive by relying on one another. Does anyone really want to be alone? Don't we all have an ancient intuition, buried deep inside bones and marrow, that human survival depends on cooperation and collaboration?

He takes a sip of his coffee and smiles, as though to say *just a second, something is missing.* He gets up and puts on a record. A rock band singing in French. A pattern is slowly increasing in intensity—setting up. He hands her the joint.

She finds herself accepting.

"We often think something is wrong with individuals, but maybe the problem lies elsewhere."

Tess takes a slow drag, which allows her to avoid responding. Then she coughs.

"So many people are disenchanted with the world as it is, because it's fucked up," he says.

This is why she liked Cam better than most other people—he didn't go on about what was wrong with the world—though he was acutely aware and fought to better it. That said, she does like Olivier's lisp. She never noticed it before. It's subtle.

"Yes," she answers.

"We're all victims of the current worldview. Imagine how different life might be, how much richer, if Europeans hadn't just stolen whatever they wanted around the world and made all the rules?" he says.

She looks around his room, looking for evidence that he has the authority to make these statements. It's not that she disagrees; it's that it's difficult for her to agree wholeheartedly to anything. She thinks something is missing: a recognition from Olivier that his frustration, and his pronouncements, are not new, perhaps? Or some acknowledgement of the accumulation of experience? Some acknowledgement of their own complicity and guilt?

She tries to imagine the future. Usually her mind turns to a little farmhouse, where she is a bohemian type of old lady with crazy hair, quilting, reading, and tending to her vegetable garden. But what if that's not her future? What if she's subject to scientific experiments, or finds herself choosing her most precious belongings in her haste to escape some kind of attack? She's always taken safety for granted, living in this country as a person with so much privilege. She wonders if she's starting to feel paranoid, but that's the problem, isn't it? Even if existential crises are familiar to millions of people, she's too naive and comfortable to expect tragedy on her own doorstep.

She can't carry a thought through to the end. The music is distracting—talking about the weather. The seasons that continue to change. The never-ending loops of happiness, sadness, darkness, happiness. Sunshine, rain, snow, then sunshine.

The song is for a woman called Marie.

Tess thinks that opinions, even ones as strong as Olivier's, might follow the patterns of the seasons. Do they come and go with time, education, and experience? Will they whirl around in Olivier's head, in circles, like snowflakes, or are they hard as ice?

She thinks maybe her mother had been some kind of activist, too. Time changed her. Maybe her mother only wore the costume of a dedicated wife and mother, though she was meant for something else. Her costume had begun to chafe. It wasn't her size. She'd occasionally take it off to rest and imagine a life where she wasn't tethered to the needs of others. Yet she was a caregiver: a wife, mother, and nurse. Did she have a choice?

"I used to have strong convictions, too," she says. "When I was younger. Like, I thought I could change the world. I also thought there would be no consequences for my actions. People didn't always share my opinions, and at some point I was too scared of rejection."

Olivier looks at her and cocks his head.

He hands her the joint again.

"Is that the worst thing that could happen?" he asks.

She shrugs and thinks that it might be. It occurs to her that she might not be driven so much by a desire to do good as by a desire to avoid being disliked.

"Why don't you have any pictures on your walls?" she asks.

"I like to paint, and if I have things on the walls, I get too distracted. It's just the way I work."

The room seems darker as a result of the smoke settling into her brain.

"What do you paint?" She hands him the joint.

"Well, I like to paint murals … " He drops his eyes.

"You didn't paint the mural outside?"

"*Ouais.* That one was fun. I took a picture of a woman in a park when she didn't know I was looking, and I painted her."

Tess has a hard time reading him. He seems to be acting coy with a measure of self-awareness, with a knowing side-eye. It's like he knows he's beautiful. As though he knows he has a part to play, and he's only playing it because he wouldn't want to let her down. Even when we think we're above certain conventions, she thinks, we still fall into patterns that bind us.

"She didn't know you took the picture?" she asks.

He shakes his head.

"And if she doesn't want her face over a wall?"

"I doubt she or anyone else knows that it's her. Every day she's at the park, legs in a sleeping bag, feeding the pigeons and talking to herself. I thought, if she is so kind to the birds, I could immortalize her. A return kindness."

Tess doesn't know how to argue with that.

"We have to look out for our neighbours," he says. He's stirring his coffee with a satisfied look on his face.

She squints to see the books on his shelf: *L'Homme rapaillé* by Gaston Miron, *On Anarchism* by Noam Chomsky, *Why I Am Not a Christian* by Bertrand Russell.

Tess notes a photo in a frame next to his desk, tucked into the darkest corner of the room. She doesn't want to get up and walk into his personal intimate space—doesn't want to give him the satisfaction of being interested in him. It looks as though he's standing with a few women. His mother and two sisters? Yes. They all look alike. Same curly dark hair and wide jaw. He's the best looking of the siblings. They're standing on some steps.

Tess leans back again. She doesn't know this person at all. She could ask him about his mother and sisters and try to find out why his father is not in the photo, but it seems futile. People collect the stories they tell about themselves, and the older she gets, the more stories she'll be expected to hear. She doesn't have the time and patience, let alone the stamina or discipline, to truly know anyone anymore.

She's already too tired.

"When I think of that woman all alone with her pigeons, I'm happy for her. Perhaps that's the life she wants to live," Olivier says.

He places his joint in an ashtray, and takes a swig of his coffee.

She realizes she may be stoned. It dawns on her when she begins to wonder if she's acting normal. If she's in a comfortable place, she can enjoy the little surprises from her mind, for example when she sees patterns that elude her during her usual, rational life. But sitting so close to a person she does not know is disconcerting.

She can't panic. She closes her eyes and breathes, and wonders whether the room might actually be like this—darker and blurrier. She senses that her perspective, though altered, might be correct. Maybe it is in the straight-edged light of sobriety that she has trouble seeing the truth.

"You delivered food to Mr. Hewitt, right?" Olivier asks, interrupting her thoughts.

She opens her eyes.

"Yes," she says, stretching her legs out. She's not ready to talk about real life. "You've been delivering to him for a long time?"

"No, he's a new client. He's quite a character though, *non*?"

"Yeah, I often find myself thinking about him," she says.

"Why?"

"Well, his apartment. It was such a mess. I wondered if he needed professional help."

Olivier has an odd expression.

"What kind of professional help?"

"I don't know. Maybe a social worker, or a psychiatrist?"

"Psychiatrie ..." he scoffs, pronouncing it in French with its unsilent *p*. "Not only do they force medication on people, but they're responsible for forced lobotomies, eugenics, sterilization ... even homosexuality was considered an illness until the seventies," he says, turning to blow the smoke towards a window in the small kitchen.

The window looks onto the back of his apartment where there is a tiny patio packed with recycling containers. Just beyond those, a rusty staircase winds downward.

What he says sounds wise, but she doesn't want to say that out loud.

"You don't think it's helpful now, though?" Tess asks.

"It's another way to control us. It's another way to make us all the same—unthinking sheep who just want to shop. Besides, I think what we take for mental illness could be a spiritual response to life. Could even be wisdom," he adds.

Tess nods, aware that he's said something important, or that he thinks he has. She's forgotten what he just said. She wonders if he has any cookies and how he knows so much about psychiatry. She wants to turn off the music.

"Could be a response to fucking unfettered capitalism. I try to imagine a world that is completely different from this one, but I can't even do it. It'll take a revolution, but people are too comfortable. As a species, we brought ourselves to a point where we have it all, and we're too blind to even see it," he adds.

He looks outside. The sun slants through the window in such a way that it lights up specks of colour in his dark eyes. She can't tell if he's trying to impress her. She can't tell if she's trying to impress him.

"I agree. We have it all. Though of course we have more than so many others. No matter how we organize ourselves, there will be people who have less, or people who need help. The world turns, has always turned, on the backs of caregivers." As often happens when she smokes, Tess feels confused, but another part of her brain usually takes over, and the words are out of her mouth before she realizes it. "I think some light can be rescued even from causes that appear doomed," she says.

Is she saying these words for the sake of conversation, or to be contrary? So many of her classmates had worn cynicism as a badge of honour; it feels nice to be optimistic.

He's sitting cross-legged and straight-backed, rolling another joint, thinking.

"I'll be right back." She gets up to use the tiny washroom. She stares into the whiteness of the sink, which has a dark, wet hair next to the drain. She looks at the sage-green tiled walls, wondering how she would have felt about this conversation two hours ago, wondering how she feels about it now. It occurs to her that she'd like to enter all the bookstores and rewrite all the history books. It seems like a brilliant idea.

She focuses. An apple-scented candle sits on the toilet. A fluffy yellow bath mat in front of his shower. Probably all purchased by his mother. The bathroom seems more opulent than the vibe in the rest of the apartment. Maybe he likes a nice shower.

So many sides to a person—what they want others to see, and what they don't. She pulls aside his grey and yellow shower curtain. A bottle of shampoo and face wash, both "made for men," and infused with manly spicy smells.

Will she end up showering with him, using these products? She's not sure what he wants from her, if anything at all. He was kind of aggressive just now, and the awkward dance of courtship is frustrating for her, if that's what it is. She doesn't know what is normal behaviour. She doesn't want him to make a move because she would resent him for it, but at the same time she wants him to make a move. She wants to feel desirable, and, despite herself, desires him.

She supposes she will have to initiate something, even if she's risking rejection or engaging in inappropriate workplace behaviour. Does it matter if she's just a volunteer? The promise of promiscuity is tantalizing: warm with desire and cold in emotion seems just what the doctor ordered. She wants someone to touch her. To keep her grounded.

Her phone makes a noise. It's in her pocket! She'd forgotten. It's a text from Jana.

Hey Tess, do you mind picking up some olive oil on your way home? Thanks, bella.

She loves that she can be useful to Jana. She still has so much to learn about her. And about Olivier. She will ask him questions. She will not falter. She'll respect and pursue the constant and perpetual mystery of life by searching for other people's hearts.

Sunshine, rain, snow, then sunshine.

Shit. How long has she been in the bathroom? When she returns to her spot on the floor, Olivier has cut up some oranges and placed them on a plate, next to some cheese slices. She is touched by the gesture. Grateful.

They eat together in silence. It's the best cheese and oranges she's ever had.

"Can I show you another painting?" he says, after a few minutes.

She nods and he opens the door. It is in fact another small, dark room. There it is: his messy double bed. The ceiling is painted black as the night sky, with one enormous star.

He stands behind her, and places his hands on her shoulders.

"Aimes-tu mon étoile?"

"Oui," she says, controlling her voice.

"I really think you're a great addition to the team."

She wonders why he brings this up as she feels his breath hot on her neck, and his gentle fingers caressing her collarbones.

"Je suis heureuse," she says. She thinks she means it.

Chapter 6

The Earth tilts.

It's expected, yet every day the darkness arrives a touch earlier, and it feels like an affront. Most people she knows love the fall, but she can't get over all the dying and the fact that people rejoice in it, in plain sight. For Tess the slanted, thinning light is a death in itself. Winds stir leaves and they rustle on pavement, and she senses stillness—the wait for the weight of the snow. It's a season that often feels like going backwards. A season of introspection, of atonement.

She doesn't need that.

She wants to be brought out of herself, to be assaulted by her senses and distracted by life going on around her, outside of her.

When she was little her mother tried to teach her to swim. She'd throw their bathing suits and towels into the trunk of the station wagon and drive to the nearest provincial park with a cordoned-off shallow section, pulling up next to the wet, foamy sand. Dampness all around. Tess was always cold, even on the sunniest days. She could call to mind the briny smell of low tide, the beach grass, pale driftwood and smooth stones lapped by a steel ocean.

The ocean had a presence like a family member, constant and uncomfortable.

She's already spending too much time in bed indulging her imagination. She expects her mind to bring her to her mother, or to Cam and his safe shoulders, or to Olivier and the ways he tried to impress her, but she thinks about Mr. Hewitt. She revisits his random questions about dreams, and wonders if he's onto something. She remembers an article she'd read about lucid dreaming: learning how to take control of one's dreams. If she can do that, then she'll always be flying. With her mother nearby.

When Tess was a kid, she knew her dad loved her. Before he retired, he'd worked as a bureaucrat in occupational health and safety. He was well-suited to office work. His thin wrists were perfect for using calculators, making photocopies, and fixing the stapler. But he tried to get out of his office as much as possible, and he'd bring Tess along.

When he took her to the water, he'd stand to the side, look-ing out over the waves, his pen sticking out of his shirt pocket, his glasses fogged up or splattered with crusted white spots. He lifted his arms to the sun and sea in private moments, when he thought no one was looking, when Tess was looking—forgiving and loving him for the display. Tess understood his longing to escape, and his envy of the lobster fishermen.

Her father knew the dangers and the challenges of the work, yet he couldn't deny the appeal of hours out at sea: escaping unpredictable emotions at home and replacing them with the unpredictable affections of the sky and sea. The dreams that cling like barnacles.

Tess shared her father's love for their crates of tiny dark mon-sters. The men would lug them off of lurching fishing boats with names like *Stella Maris* or *Mother of the Sea* painted in cursive across the sterns. She loved everything about boats—diesel fumes, the way they'd sway and bump when tied to the wharf, the gulping water lapping at their sides.

Flags or sails flapped in the wind, banging out a rhythm. Her father hung around as long as possible, checking safety protocols and asking detailed questions about the work. Perhaps he really imagined he could do it—find himself a boat and head out to the open sea. Tess didn't mind the long days of waiting. She played alone in the beached hulk near the old stack of broken lobster pots, pretending to be an explorer.

Some of her happiest moments involved running, hiding, imagining—losing herself. She imagined she was special, and someone was sending her a signal. A secret code that only she could decipher.

She couldn't go on the boats because she never learned to swim. When her mother had taken her out, she'd resisted. She'd wanted nothing more than to walk the length of the coast, picking up sandy rocks and shells, stowing them inside her pockets, wetting only the bottoms of her feet.

The tall jack pines stood inside the park. Closer to shore, the white pines seemed a little off-kilter, missing branches and leaning slightly. Their fragrance just a tease—a ribbon flowing with the ocean air. She loved them the most. Their lopsided silhouettes against the grey sky reminded her of sad people dancing. The wind tried to blow them over but never could.

She hoarded choice stones around the house, like secrets.

She didn't realize she was picking them up until her pockets were bulging.

Tess would step into the water slowly, her toes sinking into the soft sand between rocks. She'd lift her head to the clouds hanging low, like white sheets drying on the line. Then, the water would gently raise her legs up behind her, and she'd float on her stomach to believe she was swimming. She imagined she had swimmerets like a lobster.

Maybe she didn't want to get into the water because she might never be able to leave it.

Tess had been able to lie under a quilt and watch her curtains billow in the wind. She should have been more grateful. What she hadn't had, what she wished she'd had, was a family turned in on itself. Instead, they all faced outwards, searching beyond themselves, like points of a compass. Her father at work, her mother with her sadness and pride.

Not knowing how to swim felt like another failure. As an adult she'd been expected to do the following: complete university-level studies, find a steady job, and keep her father company. Eventually she'd begun losing threads of herself, unspooling, the parts of herself only loosely stitched together.

They'd each had their own escapes, but her mother had been her true north.

After she died, at the funeral, platitudes and gentle words were spoken. Tess thought her mother would have liked the light in the church. She wouldn't have wanted a fuss.

Tess wasn't able to say anything. Her father had called her up, but she just sat in the pew shaking her head. Her loss was total. Loss of the mother that was, of the one that wasn't, and of the one who would never be. She felt sorry for herself and wanted someone to take care of her. Most of all, she hated the fact that her mother's life was reduced to this—to platters of food in a church basement and a few well-meaning people who felt obliged to attend.

A random old lady at the funeral told her that it was such a shame that her mother had died young, while she was still so good-looking. Tess hadn't really realized until then that her mother was objectively beautiful, in the way of women who don't realize it: unselfconscious and unencumbered. She missed something the rest of the world could plainly see. Tess wondered if this was an indication of something odd in her mother—bad judgment perhaps, or at least a certain myopia.

Maybe all daughters think their own mothers are beautiful, like a possession. Tess supposed mothers might see beauty in their daughters too.

If her mother had seen any in her, she'd never told her about it.

Sometimes Tess has trouble conjuring her mother's voice. She wishes time could stand still as new moments continue piling on top of old moments—who she was and who she is stretching further apart—linked together only by the unreliable rope of memory.

Tess had an out-of-body experience at the reception for her mother's funeral. She saw herself, standing in the church base-ment next to the table loaded with casseroles and potato salad and pie, only she was wearing a long gown, and had shorter hair. It was a haircut she'd thought might suit her, but she'd never had the guts to go through with it. She looked older too. More sophisticated. Wealthy, even. Could this be her future self?

When her mother had died, Tess had heard her mother's voice, from a place inside, telling her not to cry. Then she saw her in the rocking chair, looking out the window. These were hallucinations to provide her with some relief—or so she said to herself.

But how to explain this vision of herself?

Chapter 7

Jana realizes that Tess is having trouble. She checks in on her and brings her books and sandwiches. Eventually she tells her to get dressed—they're going to get a coffee and a snack. She brings Tess to her favourite café. Tess doesn't notice anything about the walk, she's in a daze from having been in bed for too long. She does her best to perk up, for Jana, once they arrive. The aesthetic is an exaggerated version of Jana's apartment. Larger Persian carpets; healthy, robust plants hanging from macramé holders; dark, colourful paintings. The treats are Middle Eastern and full of honey, pistachios, and rosewater. The café offers mint tea and strong Turkish coffee.

Jana asks her how she's feeling.

Tess's mother has been dead for a year, but someone told her that in the land of grief, time works differently. In grief time can bend back upon itself, or float in a vast expanse. Tess pushes down her feelings, not wanting to feel sorry for herself. Her mother had been disgusted by too much sentimentality.

"I'm fine, just dealing with some stuff, I guess. It's better that I'm not with Cam anymore, though I miss him." That's the easiest response. She isn't ready to talk about her mother yet. "I would have relied on him for happiness and my self-esteem." Instead she was forging her own way. "But I'm really happy to be here, Jana. I'm really happy to be with you."

"That's nice to hear. You know, you're a lovely person, but I don't think you know it."

Tess is startled, embarrassed. She doesn't want a pity pep talk.

"I've been a bit worried about you," Jana says. "No, no, let me finish."

Tess sits back, feeling small.

"Do you remember when you saved that kid at my party?"

"What?"

"That time you saved the drowning kid! That short guy, what was his name? Matt? No one knew that he couldn't swim, and he was drunk, and it all happened so quickly."

Jana looks at Tess's face.

"Don't tell me you don't remember?"

"I don't remember."

"You were a hero! I think you were already in the water, and you noticed him struggling. He wasn't even making any noise, but you saw, and you pulled him out so fast."

"Jana, I don't remember this at all. I mean, I can't even swim properly." Nervous laughter coming from her own mouth. "I remember the party, though." She doesn't want to admit that it almost destroyed her with her first taste of escape, in the form of a spiked lemonade.

"I can't believe you don't remember. We all thought you were amazing."

"I find that hard to believe."

"You just seemed so sure of yourself. We admired you for that. Maybe that's why we avoided you."

Jana stirs her tea. "You know, I used to be really insecure, and I pretended to be someone else," she says.

"You did?"

"Yes, and not only in my mind. I lied to people. When I met someone new, I made up different personas, and imagined how the person in front of me might be most impressed."

"That's actually impressive," Tess says.

"How?"

"Well, you would need to be incredibly discerning, to know how people would be most impressed by you."

"I guess that's true," Jana smiles.

"It worked for me. I mean, you impressed me, so you had me figured out."

"I did it for a long time. I started it in high school. You remember all those kids at the pool party? Well, besides the one whose life you saved? They each thought I was someone different. I made up versions of myself for each person, even for you, and eventually I couldn't keep track. I wanted to tell you."

"Why?" Tess asks.

"I don't know. It's like sometimes I see glimpses of you, but then you retreat again. I know you miss your mother."

Tess nods, and takes a sip of coffee. To think she'd worried that she might not like Jana.

"Thanks, Jana. I don't know how to explain it. I feel like I'm on a rollercoaster. I want to move on and be happy, and I can almost reach it, but then ..." Tess says, as she notices two men sitting together at the other end of the café, looking at them. The men smile and nod.

She looks back at Jana. She's grateful to her, really, but what does Jana know? Both of her parents are alive, she has a close-knit family, and she was obviously raised to be confident. It seemed that nothing could be more of an affront than having one's memories questioned. If they build up and become the armour of an identity, what happens when that is shattered?

"I just can't imagine you pretending like that. So you were lying to everyone?" Tess asks, to change the subject.

"Not really lying. Just exaggerating. Trying to be what they expected me to be. Unapologetically me, or one of the fifty

87

versions of me. I think I've finally figured it out, though. Funny how it takes so much time."

Tess wishes she could say the same. How can people feel so confident about themselves?

The guys are still smiling at them. Jana smiles.

"What changed it for you? I mean, what made you stop doing it?"

Jana stirs her coffee. She looks into it, almost searching.

"I haven't yet met all the people I will love."

"Oh, that's a beautiful sentiment." Tess doesn't have the right word, and "beautiful" feels earnest and undeserved.

"Someone had posted it on Facebook—it's not mine. But I like to think about that—to think I will meet more people to love, and I want to be honest with them from the get-go."

"That's nice. I always go backwards in my mind," Tess admits.

"I do too. I miss my parents, but I know I can go home, since they beg me to, every time I talk to them."

She pauses.

"But that's not the problem. The problem is that I've already lost everything."

Tess waits, preparing herself to be understanding and compassionate for what she expects will be a minor problem in Jana's life. She won't be cynical. She can do this. She learned how to listen and ask appropriate questions. Her manner has been described as kind and warm. She'd be a good friend, just as Astrid had been to her.

Just after Tess's mother passed, Astrid had sat with her, holding her hand for hours as Tess sobbed. Tess had wanted to be comforted, consoled, and pitied. She'd wanted Astrid to feel bad for her, to let her wallow in her sadness. But Astrid had listened as Tess wailed about her mother and the fact that she'd not really known her, and now never would.

Astrid said maybe she'd begin a new relationship with her mother. A different one. Tess had been angry at first. She didn't want a relationship with an absence. She didn't want to be searching and coming up short. And how could someone who'd given her life, introduced her feet to the earth and her mouth to milk, just disappear? She'd searched and searched and finally taken herself to bed.

She's not prepared for Jana's story, though.

"Do you remember our Spanish teacher in twelfth grade?"

Tess is whisked in her mind to a desk in the front row, where she's seated in front of the man who taught her the words for carrot, *zanahoria,* and owl, *la lechuza.* So distracted was she over the bulge in his tight jeans, which rested just at her eye level, she almost wasn't able to focus on anything at all.

"Yes, Mr. García with the tight pants. What about him?"

"Well, I'm not proud of this, but we had a relationship."

"When you were in high school?"

"It started when I was in high school, yes. He was only twenty-six at the time, which I guess is still pretty old, but he seemed like one of us. Do you remember?"

Tess does remember. She remembers fantasizing about him. She fantasized about everyone at some point or another. She remembers watching other couples as they made out, wondering if she would always be alone. She watched out of the corner of her eye as boyfriends would gently move their girlfriend's hair before kissing their necks. She watched the way their hands would linger on the girls' hips, or just on top of their buttocks, or on their inner thighs. She remembers worrying that they would catch her watching. She wanted someone to want her, too.

She would sit in class, wondering if Mr. García touched someone like that. She would never have imagined that he loved a student, but it made sense that it would have been Jana.

Jana and Mr. García carried on, he was never caught, and eventually Jana was no longer his student. Later she followed him around the world when he taught in international schools. She'd spend her days painting or drawing as she waited for him to get home from work. He took her to dinner and bought her nice things. Life was exciting but also exhausting. His drive for life and fun was insatiable—it left them both empty.

Until she was pregnant.

She felt her life had finally arrived. She dreamed of a house full of all the lovely, adorable things that accompany babies: tiny socks, cribs and board books. She couldn't wait to kiss the soft baby belly and breathe in the sweetness of his breath. She couldn't believe she could be so lucky or that her life would be so full.

Mr. García, or Marcos, seemed excited too. He promised to settle down a bit. She thought, as everyone does, that it would bring them closer. And it might have.

"But my baby died before he was born."

She tries to move on, but there are days when he's all she can think about. She wants him more than she can explain with words.

"So I've been mourning the life I could have had with Marcos, as well as grieving for the baby himself. I think I've moved past the first loss, but I'll never get over the baby."

She nods resolutely, her eyes downcast.

"That's just the way it is."

Tess reaches for words while taking Jana's hand in her own. Jana's wide eyes look at her with gratitude, and no expectation.

Tess opens her mouth and nothing comes out. She feels, intimately, the inadequacy of words to express the unspeakable.

She searches for a Kleenex. People in the café shoot them sympathetic looks; the two men have put their flirting on hold. Tess hugs her.

"Jana, I have no words. I had no idea."

"How could you know?"

They slowly pull apart.

"I can't even say I'm sorry because that doesn't even cover how I feel for you. I wish there were more I could do."

"There's nothing anyone can do. I had to meditate a lot to get to a point where I could forgive myself, forgive Marcos. I still haven't forgiven the universe. I don't know. There's nothing I can do. I've never felt so helpless."

"What happened to Mr. ... Marcos?"

"Oh, the relationship fell apart. We just didn't see it the same way. He couldn't understand why I'd fallen to pieces, and I thought he seemed relieved. I don't think he was, but we just couldn't be together anymore. I think he's in Chile now, and I'm here with you. It's better that way. I don't think we would have lasted long."

Tess decides then and there to stop the afternoon naps, to stop trying to dream about her mother, to stop feeling sorry for herself. What a jerk she's been.

Jana reads her mind.

"Tess, don't feel bad that you're grieving too. We all need to heal in our time."

Tess nods. "But ... a baby." She wipes her eyes. "I never even asked you about your story."

"Even if you had, I'm not sure I could have told you."

The men are standing in front of them. They have their coats on, explaining that they don't mean to interrupt, they have to go to class, but they "couldn't leave without inviting you to a party."

They really need to invite these two crying women to their party?

Jana does the talking since Tess's mind is elsewhere. The men, young men, seem polite enough. They explain they're studying law and engineering, respectively. Their names are Daniel and Hari. They are roommates as well.

Jana is laughing now, her beautiful, raspy voice filling up the room—something the Daniel guy said. Tess finds it difficult to understand how those who have lost, really lost, move on and steel themselves for the present. Do they rid themselves of memories, or depend on them? Tess might understand why Mr. Hewitt locks himself up in his memories. Perhaps his apartment is an homage to his life.

They exchange phone numbers and the guys leave the café, jubilant. They say thank you over and over, which is a bit embarrassing, but sweet. Tess tells Jana she's going for a walk—she's spent enough time in her room for a while.

Jana gives her a hug.

Tess walks to the park to sit in the grass under the trees. Usually it is difficult for her to decide where she should sit, there are so many options, but today she feels a need to be on the ground. She has to look carefully to not sit on dog shit or cigarette butts. She finds a clean spot and wills her body to relax. The ground is cold beneath her but she doesn't mind. She breathes. The sun is in her face, and the air feels crisp.

Tess had dreamed her mother was trying to reach her. She heard a voice, distant and muffled as though traveling through water. A face appeared, crashing towards her as though riding the crest of a wave. Was it not her mother's face?

She wonders whether her mother would like it here if she were still alive. She'd like the bustle of the metro, the attractive people, the sunflowers in the market, the restaurants. Maybe living in a place like this would have helped.

Here, even meaningless interactions with strangers could be full of weight, desire, and consequences. She could make any number of connections, and have any number of interactions that might quell her loneliness—for example, with that man with dreadlocks, strolling across the park with white earbuds and a coffee cup in his hand; or with those teen girls sitting on the bench, fretting about their hair as they take selfies; or with that woman waiting for a toddler, who bends his round, little body over to point at some ants.

Tess wants to befriend them all. She wants them to notice her smiling at them. She would be whatever they need her to be. She wills them to look at her.

She takes out a pen and paper. She thinks that keeping a journal might ground her, but ends up writing a list: *Find paying job. No drinking. Be part of a team. Martial arts? Send Dad a postcard. Shop at the market. Practice French. Read. Don't think about Cam. Buy nicer clothes. Drop off Mr. Hewitt's journal. Give it back.*

A man is approaching her. He's looking right at her and smiling. She doesn't recognize him. He's about her age, maybe a bit older. He's wearing corduroy slacks and a newsboy cap. He stands in front of her, and she shields her eyes with her hand as she looks up at him.

"Sorry, Marie, I was walking home and saw you from over there, and I thought I would come and say hello. I'm Antoine. From the conference?" He speaks in French with a European accent.

She has to let this handsome stranger down, and in French. "Oh, sorry, I'm not Marie."

She smiles at him and he takes his leave. He looks disappointed and not entirely convinced. He looks back at her a few times, puzzled, as he walks away.

Lying about who she is, as Jana used to do, is tempting. Perhaps that's why she drinks. It lets her feel like a different person. It lets her move through the world with a little more ease. The feeling of being transported, swept away on a ship of memory, or invention.

That man was attractive.

Loneliness. Longing.

She wants Cam to choose her. She wants Olivier to want her. She misses Astrid, her confidence and her laugh.

She wants to stop looking for her mother's love.

She wants to be useful. Should she dedicate her life to securing a safe home for refugees, overseeing democratic elections, or teaching children who live in poverty? But then, what is at the root of that desire? Is it true love for others, or disdain for herself? A white saviour complex? Why does she believe that she, of all people, can make a difference?

Maybe Jana didn't lie about who she was, but simply felt like a different person with different people. When Tess meets people, she anticipates their perception of her, and whether she's correct or not she's faced with her own reflection: too short, too white, too inexperienced, too intellectual, too ignorant, too working class, too wealthy, too anglophone, too young, too insecure. She once asked her mother whether she might be schizophrenic for feeling like so many different people. Her mother had just laughed, though Tess had hoped she'd tell her that she's not "too" anything.

Maybe if she had, Tess wouldn't need strangers to make her feel good about herself.

Of all the people she has met, is it possible Mr. Hewitt doesn't generate any of those feelings? Is it possible he shines a light on who she really is? How odd. In fact, she can't seem to rid her mind of thoughts of Mr. Hewitt—his unseeing eyes, sad like a donkey's, and his dirty, dangerous apartment. She should help him clean it up. She should deliver food again. She'll talk to Olivier about seeing him. She'll help him; he needs her.

94

In the meantime, she has Mr. Hewitt's book in her purse. Heavy. That must be what calls to her all the time, and turns her mind to thoughts of Mr. Hewitt. She should give it back. She takes it out of her bag.

What does this journal mean to Mr. Hewitt? Is it an archive, a time capsule, or evidence that life has shape and continuity? Does hanging onto it create the illusion of control?

She knows she's going to read it, as clearly as she knows it is not her place. She's not sure why she has to read it: to find out if the existence of the journal is just a token of a messy mind? To discover all of Mr. Hewitt's memories? Maybe she needs to find out if she can piece them together, thereby reassembling the shards of Mr. Hewitt's life, like a mosaic.

It occurs to her that opening the book might be inviting the possibility of loss. She breathes in and out, counting four (breathe in), counting four (hold it), counting eight (let it out), willing the sudden longing for a drink to dissipate.

With a clear head, she rationalizes. It's a beautiful day and it's been emotional. She's been so good lately. She deserves it for trying to help others. Besides, drinking for her is not to escape her feelings. Instead, she drinks to feel more, to make sure that something will come to her—an idea or an opening. She wants to remember, and find explanations.

She picks up her things, and goes to the depanneur on the corner to buy beer.

Just one to start.

Perhaps that man would come back; she should buy two just in case.

She settles back on the grass. Now. Can she explain her deception with the truth—that reading this journal will help her to understand Mr. Hewitt? She needs to approach him in just the right way, so that he allows her to help him.

Leaning back as far as she can from the journal, she opens it, ever so gingerly. Inside, she sees big, left slanting handwriting in Spanish, mostly. Poems rendered painstakingly at the front of the book. At the back, the writing is messier, more frantic. Occasionally, she comes across drawings of birds: sparrows, storks, and owls.

She likes the owls best. Like her tattoo.

It is unclear to Tess whether this is a journal, or fiction, or whether it belonged to him or someone else. She doesn't even know where these events took place, because some details are obscured, or in Spanish. Some entries are written out in detail with dialogue like a novel, and some are in fragments, as though they are collections of thoughts. The journal seems to have different handwriting on a few pages. It occurs to her that perhaps the penmanship is the same, but the author was suffering varying degrees of fatigue, restlessness, or mania.

A date rises: *April 5*.

Then a small, worried paragraph:

I haven't written in a while, because some things should not be put down in writing. I don't want Martín to get in trouble if someone finds this, and even more importantly, I don't want him mad at me. He's my best friend but you don't want to get on his bad side.

She goes back for more beer.

La segunda parte - el verano

Bárbara stopped in front of an olive-green coloured house with a sign: *Comida caliente—todos bienvenidos.*

The room inside was painted the same colour green as the exterior, full of long wooden tables packed with people. I was struck by the quiet given how many people were in the room. Hungry people, including children and babies, waited patiently in line for a bowl of stew made by Doña Alicia.

Doña Alicia, with her enormous black eyes, a face like a moon and a ponytail down to her buttocks. She told us to call her Kiki and said she had a stew on the stove and enough food to feed about forty people. She told us, not wasting any time, to set up the serving table and dish out the food while she made a second pot in case more people arrived. I had a hard time keeping my eyes off Bárbara, whose look of stone had shifted somehow. Now her face looked open, beautiful. Sweaty.

We found bowls, spoons, and cups. Everything was made of tin. I put newspaper under one of the table legs, and we stood at the long serving table in front of the cauldrons, soup bowls, and jugs of water. When the long line of hungry people had been fed and started to head home, Kiki and her husband, Carlos, invited us upstairs to their home above the cafeteria for a cup of coffee. The house was clean and fairly empty of furniture, but full of colourful pots, vases and jugs as decoration. The clothesline ran through the window and out onto the roof of the adjoining house. Kiki and Carlos's house was one room, with a couch that turned into a bed. Cozy. Kiki and I drank coffee, while Carlos and Bárbara drank maté.

Hours passed. They said they had farmed tobacco, had ten children, but had to leave. Bárbara asked a lot of questions. I think she was trying to get information about her people too, and I felt sad thinking that she might never find them. I managed to get a few jokes in, tasteful ones, and even made Bárbara laugh.

I thought about how I'd like to capture that laugh, collect it and put it in jars around my room.

When the sun set that night, the horizon looked the colour of split watermelon. If I were a sailor, I would know the significance of a coloured sky—good weather, a storm—who knows. Right now, I'm no good to sailors, or to society. I want Bárbara's presence to envelop me all the time, but even when I'm not with her, the pain of thinking about her is delicious, because I know our separation is temporary.

I can console myself with the knowledge that she's somewhere, being herself.

The next day, I walked to Martín's house, hoping he might tell me what had happened between him and Bárbara, and to find out if I could make a move. His neighbourhood gave me the chills even though I'd grown up spending weekends at his house: the walls free of graffiti; trendy stores with expensive clothes from Europe; large houses with modern glass balconies. I rang the bell and Cecilia ushered me inside, up the carpeted steps and into the living room, where Martín stood next to his father. About ten men stood with them, in a semicircle, all smelling of cologne and cigarettes. I recognized most of them. One man, Father Pedro, wore a cassock.

I tried to turn around but Martín's dad saw me. *Puta madre.* He grabbed my hand and pulled me into him, exhaling smoke and whisky breath into my face.

"Stay for this, my boy, I think you need to hear what's coming." He hit me on the back.

Arrogant. He went back to his guests, so Martín and I started to make our way out the door, but Martín's mother, Graciela, intercepted us and greeted me in her strange, unblinking way. Her seashell-shaped eyes had always irked me a little, as had her way of speaking so softly. She was asking me what I might do after graduation, when we heard the sound of silver tapping a glass.

I thought about the nights she had come into Martín's room to tuck us in, and she tucked me in too tight. Caressed me where I'd never been touched by anyone else. A few times, her hand passed over my pants, not enough to cause any major issues but enough for me to become alert to it. Shamefully erect in fact. Bouncing uncontrollably under her fluttery fingers, while she sat there with her knowing fucking smile, wishing me pleasant dreams. I could only assume it had all been a huge misunderstanding.

For that reason, I never said anything to Martín. How in the world could I ever say anything to Martín?

His dad stood in the middle of the living room next to the record player and cleared his throat.

"My friends."

I looked at Martín and wondered if he was proud of his father. I wondered if I would have been proud of mine.

"I have known most of you since we were young men. Boys rather, just like my son here and his friend."

He gestured towards us with his arm outstretched. The men all turned and smiled at us. Their smiles were too wide and forced—whether from the drinks, the fear, the fervor.

"Together, we have worked tirelessly for our country, for our compatriots."

He looked into his glass and swirled it around.

"We have set an example for the next generation."

Martín raised his eyebrows at me.

"But unfortunately, we bear witness to a gradual mutilation of our beautiful country by those who would usurp what we have worked for all these years." Beads of sweat popped up on his hairline, and his double chin shook.

"Those who would destroy the functioning of our society with vile propaganda and immorality, and who would attempt to modify the natural order dictated by God."

I wondered how I would feel if he were my father.

"Well, my friends. The time has come for us to take on a more active role; one that requires sacrifice and careful deliberation to propel our country towards a bright and prosperous future ..."

He paused and lowered his tone, for effect.

"... by cleansing our country of filth that, if left to fester, would infect and destroy our country."

He coughed and lifted his glass. I wondered whether he might have a heart attack.

"To the Fatherland. *Salud*!"

All the men lifted their glasses and began talking at once. A few walked over and slapped him on the back. Graciela was talking to the wait staff and looking over at us from time to time. While Martín grabbed some drinks, I looked down at the table, at one of Martín's father's lighters—shaped like a revolver.

I had such a strange dream last night; I feel I have no choice but to write it down. It felt like I couldn't open my eyes but I could hear waves crashing on the shore. When I finally could see, the world had turned to black and white. By the time I stood up, in my dream, I realized I wasn't at the beach. Walls surrounded me and they were covered in shadows. Blood coursed through my ears, thick and sandy, thrumming with my heartbeat, as though I'd been swimming in the ocean.

Then I walked towards a faint light, the rhythm pulsing in my veins accompanying the pattern of my gait. Two beats at the temple for each step. As though someone were trying to send me a message.

Bárbara and I met at the bus stop to head home together. I wanted to tell her about Martín's dad and the speech he'd given, and was prepared to do so, but when I sat next to her, I couldn't. It was too heavy. I also didn't want her to know the reality of Martín's family. It would reflect badly on me.

Instead, she asked me if I wanted to go with her to the countryside for real. On a train. I asked her if it would be dangerous.

She told me to lower my voice and said we should get off for ice cream. With the bus idling between two large trucks, she yelled to the bus driver to open the door. Then she jumped down the stairs, pulling me behind her until we were ambushed by exhaust.

She took me to her favourite place where they knew her by name and she introduced me as her friend, and then we walked in the direction of the sunset with our ice cream cones. At that perfect moment, I had faith in gravity and love. Without those, nothing grounds us. You might want to argue that we're also guided by concepts such as time, language, or lust, but these are as fickle as the tides.

Once, when I was younger, I tried to create a tidal chart that would anticipate when the tides would turn. I couldn't make sense of the factors influencing the decisions of the ocean. The phases of the moon, the rule of twelfths, and so on. While it's easy to anticipate moon cycles, it is less clear how those actually affect the fluctuations of the waves. After I was told I should calculate a semidiurnal sine curve, I gave up. Sometimes an unsolved mystery is the preferred option.

As we walked together, Bárbara told me how she felt about the hypocrisy and shortcomings of society, and I responded with my poorly articulated feelings.

She said her intuition allowed her to see all sides of a story. This used to confuse her, as it became difficult to take a stand. She saw the irony, the stupidity, the ego of it all. She couldn't allow herself to act because no matter which way she turned she could see a nuanced yet logical argument against that action.

"But inaction in the face of injustice is also sinful," she said.

"But maybe people are protecting themselves? Protecting their families?"

"But why should they? No one is safe until everyone is safe. People talk about social revolutions, but it requires critical action. From all sides. We can't let our vanity and insecurity get in the way. This is not about poetry, love, and sex. This is politics and it is dirty."

She didn't yet know the power of her words, and I simply wanted to be admired. I wanted poetry, love, and sex. I would do whatever she wanted to get it.

She liked me when I listened, though she also seemed to appreciate my questions. I tried to make sure I understood her. I could never properly convey all that she was. It is so easy to see one aspect of a person and assume that is the whole. The self is not contained in a moment, or place, or even in the feelings of another. Bárbara was herself, nothing more and nothing less.

We decided to sit on a bench to enjoy the cool night air. We watched the ocean, the water bright, churning and splashing against the rocks. A thin, orange film seemed to line the horizon. I remember a palpable, tense expectation, as though a momentous event could occur at any instant—for better or for worse. I was on guard while trying to seem relaxed. I could take comfort in the fact that she was choosing to spend her time with me, but I still had many chances to mess it up. I wanted nothing more than to be wanted by someone else.

No. I wanted nothing more than to be wanted by her.

We remained silent for some time, listening. Gulls flew overhead, soaring above the water, while some clamoured around our feet, snatching the crumbs that people had dropped over the course of the day. Sitting next to her calmed me. We were sitting so close, my arm was pressed against her torso, and I felt the rhythm of her breath. Faster than mine. Her hair had a particular smell, and this time afforded me a chance to contemplate it. Like bitter cedar—I can call it to mind even as I write these words. Then she turned her eyes to me, so serious, and asked me about the topic we all thought about. All the time. She asked me if I'd ever been in love.

"Not yet," I said. "There have been some girls, but ..."

"Have you had sex?" she asked—rather bluntly, I felt.

"Uh, ha. No, not yet." The fact of my virginity, the whole, unavoidable reality of it, wasn't so awful. What was terrible was the fact that I still hadn't even kissed anyone. Not because there hadn't been anyone who wanted to kiss me (there had been at least one) but it just never worked out. I would never tell her this.

"But you've kissed someone," she asked.

"Of course."

"Tell me about her," she said.

"Well, it's more that she kissed me. She was a neighbour and we grew up together. We used to play games. Handball or whatever. Our mothers were friends. Anyway, one day we went out to buy a Coke together, and she pushed me up against a tree and kissed me. It was very sudden."

"What was her name?"

"Ana Lucía."

The truth was worse, but I wouldn't tell her that. Ana Lucía hadn't kissed me but I had placed my hand on her breast, and I'd just stood there like an idiot until someone laughed at us.

It seemed Bárbara was enjoying this. Perhaps she enjoyed feeling jealous, or protective. Perhaps it made her want me more. For me, this entire conversation was torture and I simply wanted it to end. It had actually been awful with Ana Lucía. My grandmother had seen the whole thing and never let me forget it.

"How about you?"

"Well, he was a friend of a friend." She jumped right in. "I didn't know him well, but I could tell we liked each other. Eyes that sparkled when he smiled, you know?"

I felt sick.

"We were at a party together. At some point, people started watching something on TV and he sat next to me. Then he leaned over and kissed me."

"He didn't even talk to you?"

"Of course he did, I just can't remember exactly what he said."

"Well, it couldn't have happened that quickly?"

"No. I suppose it didn't. To be honest, I had taken a seat on the couch, and he was on the other end. We were as far from one another as possible, with no one sitting in between. I hoped I wasn't too obvious, you know?"

I could feel the chambers of my heart blinking shut, wondering if they should open again. I knew who she was talking about. I knew someone whose eyes sparkled.

"Where was this?"

"Oh. Party of a mutual friend. Anyway, when my couch-partner, whom I barely knew, stretched his legs, his foot reached for mine. His unsolicited foot against my own contained an electricity that flowed up my legs and landed in the base of my stomach. I was paralyzed and could do nothing but receive his podiatric affections. While it didn't fit with any of my previous fantasies, that game of footsie was one of the most erotic moments of my life."

I was envious. I was jealous. I wanted to be the author of the most erotic moment of her life. I also wanted to be graced with her acceptance.

"I just can't imagine you like that."

"What do you mean, like, a *zorra*?"

"No, no." I had to tread carefully. "I ... would never think of you as a slut. What I mean is I can't imagine you needing anyone to complete you."

"What?"

"I just mean you're everything you need to be. You don't need anyone else."

I looked out at the plaza, searching for help. I watched the people walking by, and couldn't imagine that any of them could ever have felt this way about another person or they would never act so casual. An old woman with a kerchief around her hair made her way slowly from one side of the street to another. She took little mincing footsteps and held her purse tight to her side. A young guy in a suit slouched over his cigarette as he read a magazine. I was bursting inside. These people didn't know this feeling! So alive! I loved everyone at that moment, all these people who didn't know real love but would one day, hopefully, feel the way I felt.

Churning with emotions like the ocean water in the distance.

"You light the sea," I said.

I worried I'd overdone it, but she smiled at me, took my hand and intertwined our fingers. I turned my head and my lips fell on hers. To my relief, she answered—a sweet acquiescence. She put her hand on my cheek and I glided down into the earth, until I spread out, sprouting roots and twining them with hers. The softness, like silk. We became flowing streams merging into one. We became animals. We let our brains gently fold into themselves. Into darkness.

She had to go, and I tried to go with her. I couldn't let go of her, but she had to help her mother sew some clothes. I hoped no one would be awake when I returned home, because I just wanted to go to my room and be alone. My grandmother was in the kitchen. She'd left me a tortilla in the fridge, and had set out candles on the kitchen table. I hated eating in the dark, but knew better than to interrupt her. I also knew my mother would be hiding in her room, and I'd have to go say goodnight and rub her shoulders.

When I sat down to eat, my grandmother lit each candle slowly, one after the other. Smoke trails rose like vines up the unplastered wall as smooth and fast as her incantations. I had to stop eating because in fact this performance was mesmerizing; hair piled on her head, lips and fingers trembling, her mind a glistening spider web of spells. Sometimes her eyes rolled back in her head and she moaned. She said something about you. But I didn't know what it meant, so I didn't believe her.

Martín's navy cadet football team needed an extra player. I'm not an aggressive player, but I'm fast, and they'd asked me to fill in before. Bárbara and Mariana came too, since they'd planned a picnic that day, and they—sweet creatures—brought fruit, cheese and bread, a Thermos of coffee, and a blanket for us all to sit together after the game.

Sometimes I think my problem is that I don't have anything that I truly believe in. It seems most people I meet are of one of two minds.

At first break, I was happy to move away from the guys. I've never liked Martín's other friends much, and they gave me a hard time for being skinny. I tried to kiss Bárbara, but she said I smelled. She pushed me away, but I managed to plant a little one on her neck. She and Mariana were laughing then, claiming we should let them play, that they could beat all the guys single-handedly.

I agreed with them, but idiot Martín said "maybe if you take off your shirts to distract the other players," or something like that. I felt embarrassed for him, and almost repelled—those eyes that look inward, or beyond you, or away from you. I can't tell what it is, but Martín's sparkling eyes are shifty.

I wanted nothing more at that moment than to be close to Bárbara—to crawl into her mouth of pineapples and coffee, hide inside her curtain of hair, blur my edges in the soft spaces of her being.

I would erase myself, if she could fill me up.

Mariana shrieked. A bee buzzed around her head. Bárbara told her to stay still, but Martín stepped in between them, checking on Mariana as though he alone could save her. Mariana said she was fine. She sat down (her skirt was very short), and Bárbara waved Martín off. He really was overreacting, pretending to be a hero. But when he stood up straight, his shadow fell across the blanket like a black giant.

"Do you know she is allergic to bees?" he said.

"Of course I do, Martín. But she didn't get stung because she stayed still. What would you have done, fought off the bee?"

It's funny, I used to want to share everything with Martín. Every dream, every beautiful girl, every story, every coffee and cigarette, every laugh. But I felt my loyalties shifting right then and there, swinging like the needle of a compass.

In the distance, the cadets started shouting that the game should start.

Martín smiled—a small reptilian smile.

"I pick my battles carefully, Bárbara. A bee is not a worthy foe."

Then he grabbed a blood orange off the picnic blanket and ripped it open. Juice poured down his shirt and shorts. He winked at Mariana and ran off, calling for me to follow.

I was already drunk. We were at our favourite bar, one we'd frequented many times, but this time, it felt different. I was only going through the motions. I got drunk like a robot would, feeling nothing, just pouring drinks into myself.

So I observed people, and wrote down my observations. I normally categorize groups of people around me: there's a group laughing, men discussing some business deal, some ladies learning French. But today I looked closer. Discreetly, I watched their movements and faces when they thought no one was looking. It's strange how much you can see in people in the edges of a moment, in the wake of thought.

For example, the group laughing were two married couples, but only one man was making the women laugh. The woman married to the less funny man glanced at her own husband when the jokes subsided—perhaps to make sure he was all right, perhaps to let him know she still loved him. Maybe she wished he were funny too.

As for the two businessmen, they were father and son. I could see it now. The same forehead, the same proud jaw. Discussing a venture with another man. While they calmly discussed something in the papers, the son's anxiety was only apparent from his leg, which bounced uncontrollably.

The group learning French were old ladies with nice clothes and elegant hair. Their faces turned red when they spoke words in French, but they laughed and touched one another in encouragement. During the cracks of the conversation, though, they looked as lonely as anyone.

I wondered how I looked. I wondered if I looked like a guy who didn't feel that he knew his best friends anymore. But then, I could think of countless times Martín had been there for me: when my dog Diego died, when my grandmother was admitted to hospital, when Felipe Ávila had bullied me.

It is a complicated love, the one a young man feels for a childhood friend. I wanted to write that down, but then thought about what might happen if Martín read it, so I decided to draw. I would draw the people in the room, just as I saw them. I hadn't got very far when Martín banged another beer on top of my paper. The room darkened and I drank.

¡Loco! ¡Loco! ¡Loco!
Como un acróbata demente saltaré,
sobre el abismo de tu escote hasta sentir
que enloquecí tu corazón de libertad ...
¡Ya vas a ver!
Fucking tango.

I don't know how much time passed, but my drink was gone and Martín told me we had to go. He was in a dark mood and I had planned to sleep at his house. I think a woman might have rejected him, or someone might have insulted him, so I followed him.

Our shoes were loud on the black streets, and Esteban talked continuously. His braying laugh resonated through the narrow streets of stone apartment buildings. Someone yelled at us to shut up, but he peed on a car outside his apartment. Then he forced us into a group hug.

"You two need to kiss and make up. You both have hot girls ... how the fuck did that happen? And yet you're going home together. You could at least lend me one." His words were slurred and he laughed again, though less loud this time.

"Just go to bed, asshole."

Esteban sauntered off to his apartment, singing *O sole mio*.

We walked in silence until Martín ran to the side of the road and vomited. We had a ways to go. The city became more regal, more beautiful, more empty, as we approached his fancy neighbourhood. More than once our footsteps fell into rhythm, like when we were little and pretended to be soldiers—sometimes on the same side, sometimes not.

Martín insisted we head to the kitchen when we arrived at his house. We stumbled around until we found a light: a bright, white shock. We ate leftover chicken and rice, and then Martín was bored. He went to the pantry where his parents stocked wine and whisky. He handed me a full shot glass and told me to down it. I did. It burnt at the back of my throat, all the way down my chest.

"How about another?"

"What about you, *huevon*. Aren't you going to drink?" I asked.

"No, this is for you. To celebrate your victory. You're finally close to touching a girl's tits, even if it's over her shirt. You did touch them, didn't you?"

A fine breeze came through the small basement window. *El viento del sur.*

This line of questioning felt dangerous.

"What?"

He didn't answer, so I did the third shot, thinking about Martín and his "women." I never knew what was real and what was just talk. In a way, our relationship was predicated on these habits: he would tell me lies (or exaggerations), and I would pretend to believe him while giving him a hard time about it.

I never asked either one what had really happened between them, and suddenly I was intensely curious.

"What happened between you and Bárbara? Why are you so mad at her? And at me?" I asked, the words tripping out of my mouth in a drunken slur.

The servant walked into the kitchen—the man with white hair and a round, distinguished face. He was blurry-eyed and worried, but, when he saw Martín, his face resigned into a knowing frown.

"Did we wake you, Rodrigo? We're just toasting my friend here. He won the affections of a beautiful woman."

Rodrigo nodded and walked to the pantry. He closed a door Martín had left open, placed a glass in the cupboard and wiped the counter, and headed towards the basement bathroom.

"Do you think he hates you?" I asked Martín. I had never had servants and I always wondered what they thought about their employers. Here they were, living with people in their homes, most likely resenting them, possibly loving or desiring them, and in the end having to clean their toilets and put up with their shitty children.

Martín got an idea. He tapped me on the arm and motioned for me to follow. He placed a finger to his lips as we walked into a little room off the kitchen. Inside were a bed, bedside table, and little dresser. Very neat. Nothing on the walls save a wooden Christ on the cross. My brain struggled to catch up with my whereabouts when I realized this was Rodrigo's bedroom. Martín began rifling through the drawer of the bedside table.

"What if he comes back?" I asked.

"There's something I need to show you."

Martín opened his small dresser and took out a photo of a young girl: plump, with long black braids, sitting on a patio.

Surrounded by chickens. She was smiling, but her eyes and mouth were closed. Martín pointed at the girl and blew out his cheeks, making fun of her round face. I laughed. She did look ridiculous with her eyes closed, surrounded by chickens. It all just seemed so absurd. Who was this silly girl, and why would Rodrigo keep her photo in his bedroom? I couldn't stop laughing, but had to go to the bathroom.

I must have said so.

Martín told me to do it there, in the room. The walls started to spin. He pushed the man's pillow up to my crotch, and unzipped my zipper to speed things up. I began urinating and it was a relief, until the spray flew back onto my shirt and on the floor. Martín was laughing and I thought it was funny too. What the hell was I doing pissing into a pillow? But then Rodrigo came into the room and shouted something. Martín yelled too, because the man hadn't addressed us in the formal tense. There were shouts and things broken. At least that's what I think happened.

I sat for a long time at the boardwalk the next day, watching the ocean. For me, this watching has always felt slightly painful. The ocean is nothing if not constant movement. It is never the same.

PART III

GROUNDSWELL

Chapter 8

The words live inside her now. She lingers on certain paragraphs, and on the letters and poems stuffed into the back of the journal. She rushes through angry or defensive ones. She has the limitation of language—she learned some Spanish from Mr. García and some more in university, but she isn't able to read it all. Fortunately much of it is in English, ostensibly—and now ironically—for privacy and safety.

There's no going back. She sat there for two hours lost in another world. She wants to map out this history. She could figure out what happened to these people and try to help Mr. Hewitt heal. She's certain his problems, his isolation, and hoarding tendencies might be related to whatever happened to him when he was young. By diving into someone else's life, she could lose herself, find herself, save someone, save herself.

Service? Sacrifice? Or plain old interference?

She wants to know what happened to Bárbara, though she is apprehensive.

Tess finds Jana knitting in the kitchen, bathed in light from the window. Once again, Tess is struck by Jana's serene beauty. She looks remarkably put together, even when she's not.

Tess goes to the bathroom to gargle her mouthwash first. She probably smells like beer and she doesn't want Jana to worry.

She makes some tea.

"What are you knitting?" Tess asks.

"Baby clothes."

"Oh?" Tess tries not to sound too curious.

"I'm not pregnant or anything, don't worry." Tess is treated to Jana's throaty, sexy laugh.

"After our discussion, I didn't know what to do with myself. I decided to channel my energy into something productive, so I'm going to donate these to the hospital."

"Oh, that's great, Jana. Really great idea."

Jana nods and sips her tea. Tess wonders if she's been sitting here for long. She doesn't know if Jana's in the mood to chat, but she needs to tell her what she's done. She sits down at their small kitchen table and asks if they can talk.

Jana looks up, concerned.

"What's up?"

"Well, I just read something that has sort of shaken me up a bit. It was written by a teenager in some country in South America—I'm not sure which. It's like a journal. The writer talks about his love for this woman. This amazing love. But he also says he may have killed her. I don't know what's real."

Jana raises her eyebrows, waiting for more.

"I think one of my clients at Meals on Wheels may have written it. But I'm not sure. I don't think he would have killed anyone, but what if he did? Should I try to find out the truth?"

"What do you have to lose?" Jana says.

"It's not meddling? There may be information I don't want to know. I have no idea what's real."

"And if you ask him?"

"Well, he gave me the book for safekeeping," Tess says, "but I don't know that he wanted me to read it all." Tess looks at the table as she lies. She doesn't know if Jana knows her well enough to decipher her body language. "Besides, I won't get the information I need. He'll deflect, he'll quote philosophers, or he'll cut me out."

"Don't you think they would have found him if he'd done something wrong? He wouldn't just leave stuff lying around."

"What if it's a story, though. What if I just get myself caught in some kind of delusion?"

The next day Tess finds out that Mr. Hewitt may be delusional.

Olivier tells Tess that Mr. Hewitt has gone to the psych ward—his landlord had complained about the state of his apartment so they had sent a social worker to investigate.

"Did you see his kitchen?" he asks, as he leads her to the Tam-Tams.

"No, why?"

She can hear it already, the drums on Mont Royal, the chorus of hundreds of people banging on their own bongos. She'd told Jana to meet them there, but Jana wasn't sure she'd be able to make it. She was huddled at home, knitting, and didn't want to leave until she'd finished at least fifty little pairs of socks and hats.

"He had locked every cupboard with a combination lock, and then covered each lock with tape. He's not well, *là*. He was afraid people were going to poison him. He started refusing our food as well. I think you were right that he needed help. *En tout cas,* more help than we were able to provide."

"Is there any way I could see him?"

"You want to see him again?"

"It's hard to explain."

"Try harder."

Tess looks at him and he laughs as they arrive at the edge of the park in front of the monument of George-Étienne Cartier.

They walk past couples making out, gorgeous young people sunning themselves, and families on picnic blankets. Marijuana smoke hangs expectantly in the air and they make their way across the grassy knoll. She's surprised to see some police officers; they walk around aimlessly, waiting for something to happen. Vendors have set up stalls around the monument, selling chunky jewelry and thin, colourful summer dresses. Drummers sit directly on the monument, covering every part of it—some people perched precariously high—and the noise drowns out any attempt at conversation.

Olivier perks up as they approach the drums. She can't blame him. It's intoxicating. Hundreds of people all banging out their fervor, mostly in some kind of unison. Mostly men. A space is cleared in the middle for people to dance. An old lady in a long red dress and black shoes, like a flamenco dancer, dances with castanets. An enormous red flower crowns her white hair. Her legs barely move and her back is bent, but she is without a doubt the star of the show.

Tess smiles at Olivier, grateful to him for bringing her here. They wander a bit and decide to sit off on the side, on the grass. He puts his things down and hands her a beer. He glows with sweat—the picture of youthful masculine health. He doesn't even need to try.

"Merci," she says, wondering what he might want from her, hoping he still wanted something. They'd fooled around a bit at his apartment, he had given her a massage, but Tess hadn't felt well after smoking so much. Her brain was a dreidel inside her skull. She thought he might be the type to hold a grudge if she rejected him outright, so she told him the truth about her nausea and left before they had a chance to take it too far. The next time she arrived at the Meals on Wheels office, he acted as though everything was fine, and offered to show her more of the city.

He takes out his drum and beats it. He seems quite good, but it's hard to know. Is he following a particular beat in his head, or trying to follow the others? It's loud, and warm. He must feel her eyes on him, because he stops banging on his drum and takes a swig of his beer.

"*Ah ouais, Monsieur* Hewitt. Why the fascination with him?"

"I like him."

"Do you know anything about him? I think everyone deserves to be treated well, but that man is an asshole. He's been rude to everyone. You want to help him? You can probably just leave him alone."

He leans back on one arm. His body looks strong and flexible. She likes the jeans he's wearing today.

"I think there's hope. I think he needs someone," she answers.

"*Fait que,* you're like everyone else."

She laughs, then looks at his face.

"If people were actually given credit for how resilient they are, then people in the so-called humanitarian field wouldn't have jobs," he continues. "You can't help someone without first assuming they are helpless."

"I agree with that, to a point, but as resilient as people are, we have to show solidarity."

Is there any point stating her opinion? Who are those "people" anyway? What are they even talking about?

"It's about intention," she says, aware she's made a mistake as soon as the words are out of her mouth.

"Intention? Colonization and colonialism—all that only happened because people believed they were better than someone else. Some people say they thought they were doing something good."

"Olivier, I know that. I'm just talking about helping one person."

"It's no different," he says. "Charity, even generosity, can be a form of control. It can be more about meeting your own needs than about meeting the needs of the other person. All about ego." He points at the side of his head.

"So we should sit around and do nothing to help other people? What about you, you work for Meals on Wheels. Is that all for your ego?"

He laughs and shakes his head. Pulls out a cigarette.

"Just make sure you're not looking for an experience that will satisfy no one but yourself."

He raises his eyebrows, lights his cigarette and continues to bang on his drum.

Tess lies back in the dirty grass. She's angry and hates that he's probably right. Maybe she's too worried about Mr. Hewitt. Clouds move overhead and the earth turns. She thinks she can feel its slow spin. A Reebok sneaker hangs just above her head, its laces tied to the branch of a large maple tree. Tess stares at it. Why is it there? Who put it there, and for what purpose? Why do people have to make their mark on anything beautiful?

She thinks about Bárbara. She misses her, somehow. How could she and Mr. Hewitt have experienced such love when they were so young? She has never experienced that. Not even with Cam. What she felt for most people was a yearning, a desire to change herself through association. To allow her body to roam. To lose herself in meaning, even if it is invented.

She knows she's chasing after ghosts—other people's ghosts—for the same reason people stop to look at accidents: to imagine how other people feel; to bear witness to the fact that it is possible to survive unbearable pain; to feel concern for another and feel human, and alive, and good.

And then to go about our day.

When she sits up, Olivier stops drumming.

"But listen, if you really want to, you could try visiting him at the hospital," he says, and moves in to kiss her.

Perhaps he's just annoyed that Mr. Hewitt is all she wants to talk about.

The gift shop is located on the ground floor of the hospital. She walks through it to get to the cafeteria, and her heart breaks when she sees a couple buying a huge stuffed animal, presumably for a child. Maybe their own child. She stops in the restroom to wipe her eyes.

Laminate cafeteria tables and the salty smell of chicken noodle soup. A smooth, crooning voice on the radio. A woman in a long, caramel-coloured coat talks to a man in a hospital gown. Tess takes the elevator to the second floor. Bright lights attack from above, forming skull-like shadows from everyone's eyes. She walks past patients in double-occupancy rooms—lying in bed, sitting in straight-backed chairs, staring at walls: a tiny woman she first took for a kid, holding her arm at the wrist and talking to no one; a spaced-out teenager in bright red slippers making her way down the hall; an older woman, jet-black hair in an elegant upsweep, crying.

She tries to make herself small. Her own predictable behaviour feels like an affront.

Tess finds the reception, and asks where to find Mr. Hewitt's room. The woman behind the counter speaks to her in French. She wears a tight sweater and large earrings, as though she works for a travel agency or something—not in a bleak institutional building. The woman asks if Tess is a family member.

"No." She's not sure how to explain. She's not a friend, not even an acquaintance. "I met him through my volunteer work, and I just wanted to say hello." The receptionist looks at her for a moment too long, then directs her to the community room at the end of the hall.

It is a large room, with grey carpet and beige sofas. The psychiatry students, nurses, occupational therapists, social workers and orderlies stand out from patients by their clothes and their clear-eyed confidence. Many carry clipboards. Patients, on the other hand, look bleary-eyed, tired, and defeated. Tess wonders if people would be more likely to mistake her for a staff member or a patient. She can't decide. Coffee burns in the pot, and Tess helps herself to a little Styrofoam cup as she looks around.

She sees him. He's in conversation with a man, presumably a psychiatrist. The doctor looks the same age as the patient, but his trim goatee, clipboard, and vest contrast with Mr. Hewitt's paper gown. Mr. Hewitt has paper and pencils in front of him, though he's not drawing. What would he draw, if he can't see? Other patients' paintings are up on the walls—mostly butterflies and rainbows. Tess sits down with her coffee as though waiting for someone, yet close enough to hear their conversation.

"There is a myth, what's the name? Spirits, fairies, representing the souls of young women who died before their time, often found near bodies of water," Mr. Hewitt says. He sits very straight in his plastic chair. His gown exposes pale, bony legs and feet encased in brown slippers. His face is gaunt—a jaundiced colour—and his speech is slow, like his large, blinking eyes. He looks drugged.

"And what is it about these spirits that fascinates you?" the doctor asks.

"They don't fascinate me. You asked the question so I'm answering it."

The doctor takes off his glasses and rubs the reddened marks they've left on the sides of his nose, like tiny thumb prints.

"Mr. Hewitt, what do you want to tell us with this information?" the doctor asks, his voice gentle.

"Nothing. Nothing to say. Nothing to do. Aren't you worried, Dr. Kovacs?" He moves his head as though looking around, rubbing his pale, bony knees.

"Why should we be worried, Mr. Hewitt?"

"It's Wednesday."

It's Monday, but the doctor does not correct him.

"What happens on Wednesday?" says Dr. Kovacs.

Mr. Hewitt breaks into song. A song about days of the week on the telephone with one another. A song that probably wasn't intended to make sense, but still kind of does in Tess's mind. She would never admit that, especially not here.

"Mr. Hewitt, please focus," Dr. Kovacs says.

"Do you think you can betray someone, and not know that you've done so?"

"What do you mean by that?" Dr. Kovacs leans back, happy they're now making progress.

"Well, what if inaction is betrayal? What if you failed to act because you couldn't see the evidence in front of you?"

"What evidence, Mr. Hewitt?"

"Victor Jara was killed for his words. Words that kill. Can silence kill? Who knows? Thoreau said it's not what you look at but what you see. Maybe there was a paper."

"That is interesting, but I'm not sure what you're getting at. Was there a paper of import in your life?"

A paper of import?

"Maybe there was a paper that I didn't see. Because I can't see. So I couldn't look at it. But then, maybe I could see what was happening. Before the accident. Maybe I knew all along and didn't do anything about it. Maybe I saw it coming."

"It's easy to blame ourselves after the fact," Dr. Kovacs says.

"Yes, the gift of hindsight. What would one have done differently? Kierkegaard said life can only be understood by looking backwards, but must be lived forwards."

"Exactly. You have just read my mind, Mr. Hewitt. I think—"

"Well, we're not all as original as we'd like to believe."

"Yes, that's true." The psychiatrist seemed unfazed. He didn't even chuckle. He continued to talk in his slow, measured way.

"But what I was going to say is that I would like to understand a bit more about your life, and I'd love to know what you've learned, in retrospect."

"Camus asked how sincerity could be a condition for friendship."

"Hmm, yes. You've mentioned your friends in the past. They must be important to you. Though you also mentioned something about Wednesday. What happens on Wednesday, Mr. Hewitt?"

"People are transferred on Wednesday," Mr. Hewitt says.

"Where do they go?"

Mr. Hewitt juts out his chin like a stubborn child, as though looking at something in the far corner of the room. The security cameras are silent, patient witnesses.

"If I knew, do you think I would tell you? If I knew, do you think I'd be here? I'd be there too, if I knew ..." A vein in Mr. Hewitt's temple stands out, the same colour as his pale blue paper gown.

As he is not getting any further with Mr. Hewitt, the doctor dismisses him. An orderly comes to bring Mr. Hewitt to his room.

Chapter 9

He lies on his back, on top of the sheets, with his hands folded over his stomach. He wears the light blue hospital gown, like a re-wrapped gift. It barely covers his body, landing somewhere in the middle of his yellow thighs. Dark hairs line his slender wrists and creep up his hands.

Tess stands in the doorway for a moment.

His eyes are closed. He releases an audible exhale.

"It's rude to linger in doorways, you know."

She hesitates for a moment. She could still make a run for it.

"Mr. Hewitt, it's Tess. Do you remember me?"

"Ah, Tess. Were you the one who tried to poison me?"

Why did she come?

"No. Absolutely not. No one tried to poison you. I'm afraid those were nightmares. I'm very sorry."

"Well, which are you?"

"What?"

"Afraid, or sorry?"

Not this again.

"Mr. Hewitt, do you remember you were in the locked ward last night? Have the nightmares passed now?"

He closes his eyes and exhales.

"Do you know that trees remember? Water remembers? They locked me up as though I'm an animal, when the truth is, we're worse than animals. What we call sanity is absurd."

She can't keep up with him.

"They think reality needs to be written down to be deemed truth, right? Once it's written down, it becomes history. But what of all the alternate visions, woven through narrative? What of the spoken word? It's called a legend, or a myth. Or worse, a fable! With morals!"

Tess nods.

"But sometimes those stories make more sense than anything else. The stories of the trees. That's why I'm telling them that sanity is absurd, and no one believes me! They don't believe me that people are after me, because I made the mistake of saying the dream world told me so."

She leans against the table, and tries to keep her voice smooth and taut as the bow of a professional violinist. "Do you hear voices, Mr. Hewitt?"

"Of course I hear voices! I hear you, don't I? But how do I know you're not a dream? These damn pills make me high as a kite."

"So, in your dream—"

"Which is connected to the real world, where I know people are after me. How do you explain bullets in the ceiling? How do you explain broken glass?"

She looks around the room. Butter-coloured blinds, strawberry sheets on the bed, a vanilla sign—a reminder to wash your hands. Everything in mild, edible, pastel colours.

Tess thinks she knows why Mr. Hewitt might want to live in a dream, why he might concoct a fantasy of being wanted. Loneliness could be worse than madness.

"Mr. Hewitt, I believe our dreams sometimes reflect what we're thinking when we're awake."

"Of course it does, we talked about that. But how do you explain what I see here in this hospital? I've seen them writing in the doctor's files to keep me here." He sits up, but the process takes some time. As he swings his legs over the edge of the bed, he blinks at a spot on the floor.

"I believe that for you, this fear is real. But I also believe we see things, occasionally, the way we want to see them," Tess says.

"Well, guess what? I don't see anything. You think I want people after me? Are you daft? Who are you, anyway?"

Good question. Why on earth did she think he would want to see her? How desperate is she for companionship? Why is she trying to be like Cam?

"I'm Tess. I delivered your food, and I just wanted to make sure you were okay. I also wanted to tell you—"

"Why did they send you?"

"No one sent me."

He lowers himself off the bed and onto the floor using mostly his triceps, as one dips into a pool. "Do you think I could get a smoke break?"

"You need to talk to the nurse about that. The only thing I know, I mean, the thing I'm focused on, is that I might be able to help you."

"Help me with what?"

Tess's ears and cheeks burn. She knows from her social work studies that it would not help to feed into delusions, if that's what these are, but she feels she knows him. How to reconcile who he is, and who he was?

She wants to ask him about the journal. She wants to help him move beyond his memories, which seem to be locked in the silent objects in his apartment. She wants to see that it is possible to move away from grief.

"Well, sometimes I wonder if the truth, as you say, could lie in our memories? The past can be the present, in the sense that it is the key to everything that occurs ... presently. Does that make sense?"

"Memories! Certainly not. Each memory is a piece of a mosaic. We each have our own truth. Besides, enough people have tried to get me to 'admit' what I've done wrong. I've had enough of questions that lead you nowhere. They just get you to incriminate yourself. I know how words are twisted. Even memory can be altered with words. Nope, I've been there."

She jumps at this opening.

"Incriminate you? For what, Mr. Hewitt?"

"They feed us terrible food, as well. Not like your food. And the only person I like is Terry, the janitor," he says. "He's good. He's the only one who's good."

"Everyone is trying hard to do the best job they can. Everyone here is probably good," Tess says.

"Goodness is defined by those with power, so you don't know. Listen, why don't you read to me?"

Mr. Hewitt sits down, and she takes the opportunity to inspect him. It is odd to be in the company of someone who cannot see you. His face is long and lean, yet not unappealing.

She picks up the book on his side table, and realizes it's in Spanish. *La vida es un sueño,* a play by Pedro Calderón de la Barca. As she opens it, a folded piece of paper falls onto the ground. She picks it up. It seems to be a letter.

She doesn't know what to read to Mr. Hewitt. She wants to ask him some more questions. In the silence, she remembers something Cam told her once, something that had worked for him when he wanted to encourage people to talk about themselves. He'd found some questions online and was using them to help his clients focus on their goals, and to take control in their lives. He had asked her: *If you found out you would die tomorrow, who would you call and what would you say?*

"Mr. Hewitt, my friend once asked me this question. He would ask his clients too. He said they'd talk about how they'd call a family member from whom they're now estranged, or to apologize. Or to let someone know they're happy now."

Cam sheepishly told her they also wanted, sometimes, to tell someone they'd always loved them, someone to whom they'd never had the courage to admit their feelings.

"Seems pretty normal, no? Nothing unexpected there?" Mr. Hewitt says. So he is listening.

"Yeah. But afterwards, he would ask them, again based on this thing he read, *Then what are you waiting for?*"

A beat.

"It seems to help people think about their priorities," she adds.

What an idiot. What is she doing? This man is here in the hospital and it is possible that everyone he knows is dead. He's had a psychotic break, is convinced people are trying to murder him, and she's telling him to think of his priorities, as though he's a kid in high school?

In Cam's case, it was ill-conceived too. Most of his clients were patients with very little hope remaining. Even if they'd wanted to tell people they loved them, most of their family and friends were also dead. He was just piling grief upon grief, in the hope that people would learn to believe in ghosts.

Cam had said he wasn't a good example either, since he was still waiting to confess to someone that he had always loved them.

"Your friend is very smart?" Mr. Hewitt says, surprising her.

"Oh, well, yes. He was probably my best friend, but he's engaged to be married now."

Mr. Hewitt nods.

"But it's okay. He's better off that way. But he was always kind, and good, and there for me, especially when my mother died."

Tess thinks of all the times he tried to tell her. That one time they shared a bed after a drunken night and he hugged her all night. How many drunken nights had they shared? She said his name a few times and tried to wake him, but his arm over her waist was a dead weight. She only realized later that he had been pretending. He was willing to risk his pride, or rejection, in order to embrace her at least once.

"It's impossible to guess at one's own motives in the throes of grief, let alone those of others," Mr. Hewitt says.

"Yeah, maybe I wasn't in the right place. Or, right place, wrong time. He put up with me for as long as he could, but I guess he gave up. I miss him."

"And you think of him now, so he's still part of you."

Tess smiles. Who was helping whom?

Perhaps she wasn't wrong in coming to visit after all.

Chapter 10

Tess is in the kitchen preparing roast chicken and potatoes. She hates touching raw chicken, but it's Jana's favourite meal and Tess wants to do nice things for Jana. She cuts carrots and mushrooms for their salad, and opens a bottle of wine. As she drinks, she sings, and wonders what music Jana would have played for her baby. She thinks maybe she should make a mixed tape for this baby who sparked to life inside Jana, perfect and complete. The child who decided not to stay. The child whose entire life was magic—who knew the mystery of before and after, with nothing but a brief interval on earth where he embodied expectation and hope. She wonders what music you play for someone who is nothing but love.

Her phone rings and she's brought back to the salad dressing. Cam.

She looks over at Jana who is working on her laptop. She picks up expectantly, excited to hear his voice and his casual, slow, "All right, Tess?"

But his voice is muffled, slurred.

"Cam, what's going on?"

Perhaps her voice is slurred, too. She picks up her bottle of wine and it's already almost empty.

"It bothers me that I can't picture you there. I don't know what you're doing or who you're with. I don't know if you can see trees from your room."

She laughs, even though he sounds so serious.

"It's like you've disappeared."

She'd thought theirs was a friendship more pure than romantic love, and should not be tarnished by greed or jealousy or lust.

Tess says something about being busy making dinner while grappling with the feeling of wanting to nurture, chastise, and love him. He's drunk. She wonders if he drinks with Rita, or just on his own. She knows that to listen to Cam in this state would only bring her back to that unpredictable ocean where she floated in wonder, jealousy, self-loathing and insecurity. Besides, she's drunk too.

Despite herself, she asks him why he cares, as she hides her empty bottle in the recycling bin.

His voice is muffled again, as though he's gripping the phone—covering the mic. At times his volatility would get the best of him and he'd find himself arrested or beaten up, especially when he'd drunk too much. He could fly into a rage, but it was always for what she would have considered the "right" reasons. On behalf of others. To protect others. He could always find a way to get into people's good graces. It was his heart.

"Since you left ... it's like ... now that you're gone, I don't know. I mean, do you fit in there? Do you even speak French? Are you coming back?"

This is what she wanted him to say, but now that he's said it, she doesn't feel better. She wants to tell Cam that he sold out. He's doing all the things he swore he'd never do, like settle down. Should she be disappointed that he's not living the life she thought he should live? She looks out the window and the reminders that she's inland—the absence of a true horizon, a jagged sky.

Far from the sea, but still with a river. A vein.

She wonders what is worse—holding onto hope that a person might come back, or accepting that they're gone. Do we ever accept it?

"I'm not coming back, Cam. Not yet, anyway," she says. "How is Rita?"

"She's pregnant."

Mr. Hewitt's social worker from the hospital, Noah, deems the apartment unfit. He decides with the doctors that Mr. Hewitt needs to live in a group home, and Mr. Hewitt doesn't know yet.

Noah has told Tess first. He agreed that she could help Mr. Hewitt move after she told him that she completed a degree in social work and is on friendly terms with him. Tess doesn't like Noah much—he seems happy to turn the file over to her for her free labour. But he does give her information about the requirements to join the provincial order of social workers, and he offers to pass out her resume to some colleagues in the field.

She brings Mr. Hewitt back to his apartment to choose what he might want to keep. Outside the crisp air cleans the stale film of the hospital from her skin. Objects look sharp, colours appear bright. They walk for some time in silence—Tess observing the trees, their leaves red and bursting with the life that will soon leave them, and Mr. Hewitt's face pointed towards the universe of the ground. He has agreed to take her arm, and to let her lead him.

They walk through this eclectic part of the city, where subsidized housing, *centres sociaux communautaires*, and mosques mix with synagogues, Greek restaurants, and university students. People hustle by to catch a bus or the metro, to buy groceries or go to the bank.

Tess thinks about the trade-offs in coming to a new country, province, or city. Have all these people reconciled with all their losses? Which parts of their identities did they leave behind? Did they leave behind daily rituals that are impossible to recreate, favourite snacks that they can't find here, special spots where they hid or felt safe as children? When they hear a melody that reminds them of home, does it stop them in their tracks?

Tess has prepared a list of questions to ask Mr. Hewitt as they walk. A simple one to start.

"Mr. Hewitt, how did you feel when you first arrived here?"

He turns his face to the sky. They're about the same height, and Tess observes his profile. His skin is sagging around his ear lobes, and he has small pimples under the stubble of his sideburns. She wonders how he shaves. His scalp looks itchy, and his skin is pale, but she is certain that he would have been handsome as a young man.

"Do you hear that? It's a blue jay," he says.

"Oh yes, I can see it."

"Do you see a u-shaped black collar around its neck?" he asks.

"What does that mean?"

"In blue jays, both sexes look the same."

Is he avoiding her question? They shuffle along.

"You know a lot about birds, Mr. Hewitt?"

"Only some blue jays migrate, others stay in place. I always thought that people who stay in the same place might lack some kind of imagination. Simple-minded, you know. Afraid of discovery. I always liked people who could confront the unknown. I like people who seek out that kind of discomfort."

"Yes, I feel the same way."

"Ah, but be wary, my dear. It is by universal misunderstanding that all agree, for if, by ill luck, people understood each other, they would never agree. Baudelaire said that."

"Oh," Tess says, unsure how to respond.

"Maybe you don't understand what I mean at all. Though he also said we've all been touched by the wing tip of madness."

"That I understand."

"You know blue jays mate for life?" he asks.

Tess decides to take a chance; the day is so beautiful and Mr. Hewitt is in a good mood.

"Mr. Hewitt, do you think about your past, or ever wonder how you might have done things differently?"

She regrets the words as they leave her mouth. Maybe forces beyond his control circumscribed his life and he was not left with any choices. Mr. Hewitt chews his cheek, thinking, until he finally says, "My grandmother used to look forward. Ahead. She always said the past was a predator."

"She's right."

"What are you running from, my dear?"

"Well, a few things." She laughs for no reason. "But my mother died a year ago and, well, in a way I'm trying to figure her out."

"Ah, yes, the bruised lily of grief. Life is a series of tender goodbyes. They leave, and we search. But they are lost to us. They can't tell us where they are. They may reach out and make their presence known from time to time. The ultimate mystery. Do we want to know the truth? And then we have our own final exit. *Los amigos, en el tabaco, en el café, en el vino, al borde de la noche se levantan, como esas voces que a lo lejos cantan, sin que se sepa que, por el camino.*"

"That sounds nice, Mr. Hewitt. What does it mean?"

He begins coughing and asks her for a cigarette.

She tells him he can't.

So many older people she knows seem to speak about the mundane or the truly exceptional, about the weather and winter tires, punctuated with the occasional proclamation about time and space and love. Maybe it has to do with the way our memories function—the liminal space where they exist alongside imagination. Maybe it has to do with the accumulation of knowledge. Maybe it is a natural destination for most people to reach a point where only the two extremes make sense, leaving the noisy middle part for the rest.

"Where did you used to live, Mr. Hewitt?"

"I try to forget that life," he says, and takes a breath that reminds Tess of a petulant child.

"That life was worse than this one?" Tess asks, louder than she'd intended. Jesus, she's going to be a terrible social worker. Fortunately Mr. Hewitt doesn't seem to hold it against her.

"All I remember is that I arrived here and I thought the world had turned upside down. Different seasons, different stars at night. Everything topsy-turvy," he says, and laughs. It sounds like a car over gravel.

"That must have been difficult."

"Ha! Difficult ..." He shakes his head.

She imagines Mr. Hewitt as a young man again. "How old were you then?"

"I must have been about twenty-one, twenty-two? I didn't have any friends or anything to do, so I'd go out and walk. Moments bookended by nothing, while I waited for something. I must have walked hundreds of kilometers."

"And you couldn't go back home?" she asks, hesitantly.

"No. I couldn't. That was impossible."

She's silent, sensing he might say more, but they arrive at the steps of the apartment. Mr. Hewitt gazes up toward its windows.

"The past really is a predator, Tess."

Chapter 11

She would have to agree that the past is a predator. Her own past was murky, and if she thought about it too much, it threatened to swallow her like quicksand. When she was little, Tess thought she might die when she was sent away to stay with her aunt in the country—those summers when her mother needed a "rest." She hated the sun blinding her eyes, the dirt under her nails, the flies. She hated the constant smell of mould, the hard mattress, being forced awake early in the cold, and lying awake until late at night. She hated the sounds around her, the nocturnal animals, the whoosh through the trees and the haunting calls of birds, the heavy-throated frogs and the muffled noises of the other people in the house.

Most of all, she hated thinking that her mother might be lonely without her.

Even when she was alive, her mother felt like a memory. She'd never been present enough to seem real. Tess looked for her in stone and clay—she tried to mould her with her bare hands, but she was a wisp of smoke. Her aunt tried to explain. She said her mother was visited by a black bear who would sleep inside her all winter, hibernating in her body. Tess couldn't wait until the spring, when the bear would leave her mother alone.

Sometimes worry could feel like a prayer.

She'd been so painfully shy and hesitant as a child. Her parents had done their best, she supposed, to instill in her a sense of security, only to remove it once Tess seemed too confident for their liking. They thought it was their duty to take her down a peg or two.

At Jana's pool party, after years of stuttering, stammering, lowering her eyes or averting her burning face, she discovered all that was beautiful and true. She felt glorious when the spiked lemonade flooded her veins like an elixir of strength. She was invincible as she strode through the pockets of people at the edge of the pool. She searched for and found attention, love, and satisfaction.

She'd been so arrogant, so extreme, moving from one version of herself to another. She'd finally learned to take up space, until it was too much space. All she'd ever wanted was for someone to find her and love her.

Later, in her bed, she wondered how this apartment might seem if Cam were here with her, their arms wrapped around one another's bodies. Would she feel safe and home, or would they both feel like imposters? Maybe she only loved Cam out of convenience. Maybe he was in the right place at the right time. Or maybe she'd never find anyone as glorious and safe as he. Thoughts of Cam urged an unexpected ache towards her lower belly. Despite herself, she thought of home—the stones in her suitcase, the objects people hold onto to remind them of themselves. Some cling to junk, like Mr. Hewitt; others to a sense of righteousness, like Cam; still others to unrequited dreams and bitterness.

Once Cam was no longer just a friend, and she knew the feel of his touch, the lines of his body, the low, private sounds that came from a deep, secret place, she was nudged into a truce with impermanence. She'd wanted to pretend their relationship was platonic—based on a mutual desire to absolve their own guilt by fixing the world's problems. But he'd poured her drinks and they'd walked together through the trees pretending to look for beaver dams even though they knew exactly what would happen.

Perhaps the moon and the starlight, the night shadows and the ebb of the nearby ocean made their reactions to one another feel more natural, phenomena that just couldn't be helped. They were pulled in by the tides.

Maybe she shouldn't feel guilty. Maybe she's also losing her grip on reality. She feels she's travelling with two young people, on a train, looking for a family and rooting out injustice. She's being led around the places that made her bones. She's in bed and a man's breath touches her neck and she arches her back to meet him. When she opens her eyes, there's no one there. Not in a physical sense, anyway. She sees the vastness of the sky and imagines she can fill it with her love. It is blue like a robin's egg.

Tess knows she's been going through the motions. She has to stop counting the days since her mother died.

Inside, she's grateful for her warm jacket and gloves. The heat has been cut. It is colder inside now than out; a dead mouse lies frozen to the floor. She understands why the landlord was upset. She watches Mr. Hewitt, searching for some reaction to his environment, to the smells at least, but his face remains stoic, blank. She can't reconcile his gentle, thoughtful presence and the odd clusters of objects around him.

"Do you have an idea of the kinds of things you'd like to keep, so I can help you look for them?"

He shakes his head. Pale sunlight slants in through the window, illuminating cold dust skating through the air. Tess walks to a box of papers and looks inside. She's confronted with the stifling feeling of the hospital. Many pages are blank. Some have a few lines scribbled diagonally or in zigzags across the page—the same handwriting she'd found in the journal.

She wonders, suddenly, whether he might look for the journal.

"Tess, let me ask you something," Mr. Hewitt says. Her stomach jumps to her chest. He's seated on a stool, a bag of clothes next to him. It seems he has already chosen what he wants to keep.

"Do you really think I'm too sick to live on my own? Can't you talk to those doctors?"

"I think you were very sick when you lived here, and I believe you'll be happier and safer in a group home."

"What is your home like?"

"I have a nice apartment with a woman I used to know in high school. And her cat, Ingrid."

"Ah yes, the cat. Borges called it the magical animal that lives in the eternity of an instant. Unlike us, poor creatures. We can conceive of different realities but we're bound to keep making the mistake of regretting, romanticizing, or antici-pating. Don't we? We don't realize that we're shackled to one moment at a time."

She barely registers Mr. Hewitt's words. Inside one of the boxes, she notices a lighter. It is metallic, shaped like some kind of gun. She remembers the journal mentioning a lighter shaped like a revolver. Martín's father's lighter. Why would Mr. Hewitt have it?

"You know, we can write ourselves through time, through a maze, and end up back at ourselves," he says.

"And who are you?" she asks.

Mr. Hewitt turns his face to the small window.

He seems to relax when he hears the birds. She decides she should follow her client's example as the first step in her plan to start living—even if he can't see it, or see all of it, he focuses on the magic that slips in and out of the day. Words can describe the smell of a forest, or the light cast by a sunset, but there's also the intangible, which she thinks she might learn to sense, or even cherish, if she works hard enough.

Is it a good thing, she wonders, when we have it so good we have to remind ourselves constantly to feel grateful?

Mr. Hewitt walks towards the bathroom, and she hesitantly places the lighter back in the box. She takes a deep breath and quickly sifts through papers, which now seem damp. More drawings of birds and pages of writing, then a thicker piece of paper.

She checks for Mr. Hewitt—still in the bathroom—then gingerly turns it over. It's a black and white photo of a woman, probably in her twenties. She has long, straight dark hair and black eyeliner highlights her eyes. Her teeth are slightly crooked and exposed in a faint smile, though she appears serious. She stands in a kitchen reaching for something from a cupboard. Her expression towards the camera, or the photographer, is a mixture of surprise and affection.

Tess holds the photo, waiting for Mr. Hewitt.

When he comes out of the bathroom, she asks him to check whether he wants to keep anything else. They move quickly around the apartment together. She guides him and they avoid the dead mouse.

Then she places her hand on his arm. Hands the photo to him. Describes it. He clamps his mouth shut and looks away, far away, until a hoarse laugh escapes his mouth. The woman's photo slips from his grasp and parachutes to the ground. He bends down slowly, immediately, to retrieve it.

He hands the photo back.

"You don't want to keep this?" she asks. She suspects this is Bárbara. She wants to ask, but he'll wonder how Tess knows about her. He never mentioned her.

"You can keep it for me."

"Mr. Hewitt, do you want to take some more time here? Maybe there are more photos, or things you'd like to keep? If you don't take them now, they'll be disposed of forever."

He shakes his head.

"Nothing but shards of memories here," he says. "We're surrounded by objects expressing the oddity of our own temperaments. Besides, if the people you love are gone, what's the point in keeping their things?"

"Strange. I always say the same thing. Except that I have held on to a few of my mother's things, because I can't let them go."

"We surround ourselves for comfort and protection. The past keeps me safe. I will never again live something so terrible. Or wonderful. A reminder I'll never make the mistake of needing someone again."

"But we always need someone, don't we?" Tess asks.

"Yes, isn't that the sad truth, for people like us? We want to be alone, yet we can't."

She wonders how he knows that about her.

"These boxes contain violence. Violence of words. Actions. Objects. Violence of inaction."

"What do you mean, Mr. Hewitt?"

He opens his mouth, but the words are caught. He glances away, at the window.

She doesn't want to press it. What seems like a lovely photo to her might be too painful to bear for Mr. Hewitt. Nostalgia can feel so lovely, but it is dangerous, for both communities and individuals. She saw her mother fall under its spell, unable to escape her own mind and the memories locked inside. Like a little snow globe, she'd shut them up and shake them to help her get through the day. Tess never figured out what those memories were.

"I hear a nuthatch," he says.

Tess touches his arm.

"If you don't mind my asking, what is this woman's name? She's beautiful."

Mr. Hewitt looks back at Tess, his face slack.

"Love is so short, forgetting so long ..." he says. "That's Neruda. Isn't he right?"

Tess takes the bus home. She's too drained to walk and she doesn't want to go underground. It would take about an hour to walk anyway, and she wants to be home in time to cook dinner for Jana. She's full of questions, but most of all, what happened to Bárbara? How can she get Mr. Hewitt to talk about her?

She looks at her phone for a rest. For a distraction. After checking all her notifications, which she may as well not have checked, she sees a text from Astrid.

I saw your dad today.

She has a missed call and a voicemail from Cam.

"Hi Tess, um, just wanted to let you know that ... you might want to talk to your dad."

She panics and texts them both. *What's going on?*

She tries to reach her dad with no luck. She emails her aunt, but it's the wrong email address. She receives a snarky email almost immediately, telling her how sad it is that she doesn't know her own aunt's email address.

Why don't people have better things to do?

She calls Astrid again.

"Tess, I'm not sure what to tell you. I saw your dad in the pub the other day with a young woman who looked just like you. Except she wasn't you. Obviously."

Tess is relieved. How does this qualify as an emergency that two people have to write about? So her dad has made a young friend. So what?

Then she remembers.

"Wait, did she have short hair? Like that cute cut I always wanted but was too afraid to get?"

Like the woman at her mother's funeral.

"Uh, I don't remember her hair that well. I just remember she looked so much like you, it was freaky. Also, he was crying. I don't know if he's dating this person, or if he misses you and is hanging out with her for that reason, but I think you should talk to him."

"He was crying?"

"Yes."

Her dad was a softie, but he wouldn't cry with a stranger.

"And what was the woman doing?"

"It looked like she was comforting him."

La tercera parte - el otoño

Bárbara passes me notes in the hall. She writes to me in Italian, and draws leaves in the margins. Her handwriting is small and neat, except for her name—her Bs are big and round, and I imagine she's been writing them the same way since she was a little girl. She's joined a group of student journalists and wants me to join. I'll do it. I'll go back to the shantytown, I'll go to her meetings. When I see her coming, I intentionally slow my thoughts so I'm focusing only on the sensation of her hand in mine. Her hand never lingers long, but the feeling does.

With the notes, she tells me where to meet her.

On a day as bright and crisp as a painting, only one seat remained on the bus. We were headed to buy train tickets. Bárbara made herself comfortable on my lap and the old man next to us mumbled "*puta madre* ..." and insulted us. We ignored him and I reached my arms around her waist. She caressed my arms and repositioned herself on my lap, so she'd know how I felt about her. I ached to be alone with her.

The bus lurched to a stop to let an old woman off the bus. Then three well-dressed, polished men in suits marched up the stairs—straight backs and shiny shoes. They grabbed a woman who was seated near the front, a woman in a long olive-green skirt with a bag of groceries on her lap. I hadn't noticed her until she let out a scream the men didn't bother to muffle. One of the men grabbed her arm and another pulled her by the hair. I felt Bárbara rise slightly off my lap as though she'd run after them.

The woman's bag of groceries tumbled over, its contents spilling across the aisle. As the bus turned, a jar of baby food rolled back and forth, knocking back and forth across the bus and against people's feet.

No one picked it up.

We decided to go back to see Carlos and Kiki in the shantytown, and spent the day serving food. When we'd finished cleaning up, Kiki and Carlos invited us upstairs, where we watched Carlos eat a mango with a knife.

"What do eating mangoes and sex have in common?"

We shook our heads.

"You end up with hair in your teeth!"

I didn't dare look at Bárbara, and thankfully Kiki just offered us food. She mentioned they'd be hosting a party to celebrate a wedding in the villa. I wasn't sure it was an invitation, but Bárbara said she'd love to stay.

At the start, I'd come here for one reason alone: to be near Bárbara as much as possible. Today she wore a yellow shirt as she mopped in the kitchen, and we circled her as though she was the sun. I was in charge of cutting potatoes. I realized that I also like doing this work.

We were placed in charge of decorations. We didn't have any materials, but Bárbara found some toilet paper and hung it up like streamers around the canteen. I felt like a kid as I made toilet paper flowers and placed them around the serving table. It was being transformed into the head table for the bride and groom. Bárbara told me she loved my hidden talent. At one point, she stopped near me and leaned in to kiss my eyelid, so soft.

People arrived then, bearing small gifts of soap or fruit. They looked dressed up. We greeted and seated the guests as Kiki and Carlos worked in the kitchen, preparing dinner and cake. A man arrived with a crate of alcohol, setting up a bar in the corner, while another group of men set up their guitars, a drum, and a flute.

The bride and groom sat at the head of the table with Kiki and Carlos next to them. The bride wore a beige dress and her long black hair tied in a bun, and looked beautiful. I wondered if the groom felt the same about his bride as I feel about Bárbara. They were so lucky.

The band struck up a song that everyone seemed to know except for Bárbara and me, and the newlyweds danced together for a while alone on what had become the dance floor, whispering and laughing. I put my arm around Bárbara. She kissed my cheek.

She said my name with such tenderness.

Afterwards, we stayed to help clean up, and Kiki and Carlos finally opened up. Maybe it was the booze, or the good vibes generated by the wedding, but they explained to us why they'd moved to the shantytown.

"We lived a hundred kilometers outside the provincial capital. We farmed tobacco. The children helped us in the mornings. In the afternoons, they'd go to school."

They held up a photo of their children. Kiki stood in front, her arm around a girl of about twelve. Other children of varying ages were sitting or standing in front of the house bordered by a patio, some orange and lemon trees, and bougainvillea. A beautiful place to live. They looked happy, even if they were poor. A young man stood in the back with Carlos, squinting his eyes in the sun.

"We faced many difficulties. However, at that time, *chacareros* could still survive by farming tobacco. After the harvest, we could buy a mattress, a chair, in good years even a bed frame."

Their provincial accents became more pronounced as they reminisced.

"We could feed our family. Others had to buy food and other staples from their *patrones*, who charged a high interest."

Kiki and Carlos kept picking up the story where the other had left off.

"Farming tobacco is back-breaking work. The growing season is longer than a year. We have to cradle the tiny plants into the ground, tend them individually against insects, and then pick them leaf by leaf, with our hands."

"We were happy to do it when we were paid enough and left alone. We worked for twenty years for the same *patrón*, raised our children, but then were thrown off the land. After paying the owner 50 percent of the harvest every year."

"It was the same story everywhere. People who wanted to own the patch of land they'd been farming were told they were not allowed. The land is owned by a handful of interrelated families, who live in Paris or somewhere."

"And the government started buying light American cigarettes, not even supporting the tobacco farmers here."

I began to yawn until they mentioned that their son, Antonio, had been detained for eight years because he organized tobacco farmers for better conditions and pay. Antonio's wife had been tortured and thrown from a truck. Kiki and Carlos said they felt safer in the shantytown.

With each word uttered, I felt myself grow smaller and smaller. Guilty somehow, as though their difficult life were the direct result of my easy life. As though everything I had had been taken directly from someone else. A zero-sum game. Suddenly the pride I felt at chopping a few potatoes didn't feel so good.

Eventually, I couldn't keep my eyes open; the night was already dreaming of morning. Kiki and Carlos insisted we sleep in their bed. They said they'd go next door, said their neighbours had room. We resisted a little but I think we knew they wouldn't take no for an answer. Besides, we got to lie together for the first time—Bárbara next to me, looking me in the eye—her beautiful and determined face in front of my own.

I could see the woman she would become, could imagine the lines that would form around her eyes. We wanted to be as brave as Kiki and Carlos. The thing I understood, then, was that Kiki and Carlos could do just about anything, if they felt even a fraction for one another what I felt for Bárbara. I wanted to do something great. For her.

We pack. She brings a gun. We take the train because it is poetic, and we pretend to be on our honeymoon. Bárbara could remark on the smallest things. Nothing goes past her without some kind of observation. She is aware that she's equipped with insufficient knowledge, and it maddens her.

She wants to see how people are living—to see for herself. We stop at restaurants for truckers, they have warm soup and cold beer. The restaurants are decorated with clocks, a calendar from last year, a photo of a football team, a saint. We eat steak and drink wine with soda water. We meet people with Armenian, Hungarian, German, Italian and Welsh last names. Leather jackets. Leathery faces.

Out the window we observe the flat roofs of solitary houses. They're made of mud blocks or bricks, with clotheslines strung up across a never-ending expanse of a rich blue sky. Pregnant dogs sleep on the side of the road. Chickens hop about.

Occasionally, on the side of the road, an apple stand, where a woman sits expectantly with a preteen girl, wearing matching green aprons.

We travel north, until the air no longer holds any moisture. The dry density of ancient beliefs whispers through the sand, landing in my hair and eyes and settling on my shoes. She walks on and on, and I keep up. I circle like a condor. I am soaring. We see marks on a stone said to be constellations as observed by the Indigenous people in this region, hundreds or thousands of years ago. The sand is darker than I imagined it would be, like rust. It covers everything, including the hills and rocks. Full of minerals and salt.

I am afraid of heights, but I breathe.

We come to a plaza and sit on a bench. A stray dog rests at our feet, while a man and woman with dirty grey-black hair sell jewelry and single cigarettes. Her needs are not many; I want to fulfill them all. A girl nearby begins to sing while she plays guitar. She wears jean shorts, and she's added sparkles to the sides of her starburst eyes. Her hair is short and black and she sings about searching for joy. *Alegría.* We move to the patio and order two beers. We drink them quickly. Then we order two more. They are smooth and refreshing after water that tastes like salt. We are thirsty. Parched. Bárbara says we should stay here overnight, and I don't argue.

She asks me about Martín. I don't tell her that I'm slightly fearful of the pleasure Martín takes in causing others pain. He has always been my best friend. What does that mean? The friend you like the most, or the one who knows you the best? His father helped my mother. His father taught me how to be a man. I am indebted to Martín. I am cemented to him. Maybe we are one.

But Bárbara and I seek each other out in the dark, brushing sand out of hair and off of skin as we come together. It is cold and dry, and it takes some time for us to warm to each other's touch. Love ribbons around us and we either open ourselves to it, or we don't. It moves through my cells and rolls off my tongue in words, like the slanted, windblown trees that rise up into the mountains. She tells me that she can't imagine a life that doesn't include me; she lets me touch her everywhere. I can't get enough and we move together to release the chill in our bones until we have melted like glacial streams. Finally warm.

My grandmother told us she'd had a premonition. She said the city is going to be filled with dangerous creatures, like crows, who will attack us from the trees when we're not looking.

My mother was washing dishes and overheard. She told my grandmother to keep her crazy old lady stories to herself. My grandmother insisted, though, which she rarely does with my mother. My mother is too rational, too clinical in her views of the world. Predictably, my mother said that she hadn't heard anything on the news about dangerous birds coming to the city. My grandmother said just because she hasn't heard it doesn't mean it's not true. My mother said she believes what she sees. My grandmother said my mother sees what she wants to believe.

Then my mother forced a plate down so hard it broke in the sink. She held a tea towel to her bloody palm.

"Listen to me. I won't stand for it. The government is doing its job. Now I never want to hear either of you speak of this again."

Sand, dust, and dehydration.

We remarked that we'd begun our journey on a crowded bus full of elegant people and ended here, at the end of the world. Nowhere. We were no one. It was here, with her, that

I felt my first attack. The vastness of the sky, combined with the immensity of my feelings for her. An intuition that maybe even the young have, that it will never get better than this. It is all unsustainable. It will end soon. I had to breathe. I had to sit. She helped me. The air felt sharp in my lungs as I breathed in. She seemed frightened.

She'd distributed money and books to hundreds of families. I was just along for the ride.

I think she also had an ulterior motive. Maybe she thought she'd find her family. I'm not sure how she thought she'd do it, but she was convinced she'd recognize them when she saw them. I saw her scrutinize every person we met, looking for some hint that they might be kin.

When we got back to the city, Bárbara moved out of her mother's apartment. A huge mansion was renting out sheds in the garden as rooms. She lives with Juan Pablo and Antonia. She claims she moved out to protect her mother. To protect me. When I met them, I could tell right away that Juan Pablo didn't like me, or didn't understand why Bárbara would like me. He must be after her. He is her type. Handsome, smart, principled. They have a closet full of guns. She says she feels nothing for him. I should believe her. I bring her pistachio ice cream and we make love on her bed next to the window. I imagine Juan Pablo can see us.

I imagine him being jealous.

At home, in bed, wherever I am, I try not to think about her so much. It seems the more I think about her, the more my thoughts turn her into thoughts. She loses her substance, and I'm faced with a shadow. No one can stand being thought of that much. I try thinking of other things. A boat rocking in the harbour; the incredible roundness of a drop of water; steam on my bathroom mirror; my face this morning, blurred at the edges. What did my face look like?

Sometimes I feel like two different people. As if I'm living two different lives.

I wonder if I'll enter her dreams?

My mother says to slow down, that I'm too young. My grandmother says it's cruel that I didn't meet her later in life. All I know is that I hope to still be with her, then, holding her hand even when the skin is soft and papery.

After school Martín told us to come to his house. His parents were entertaining, so we sat in the garden with Esteban while the waiter—not Rodrigo, he'd been fired—brought us glasses on a silver tray. He poured our whisky and offered us bowls of olives with little white napkins. I felt terrible, knowing Rodrigo had been fired because of me.

I asked Martín where the new waiter was from.

"The waiter?" Martín said. He looked at Esteban. "*¿Que sé yo*? Who the fuck cares?"

"Why do you want to know?" Esteban asked, leaning back and taking a slow drag of his cigarette, his index finger curled around the top. His long legs were spread open wide and he filled up the flimsy plastic chair with his large body.

"I don't know. I suppose lately I'm thinking more about where people come from and end up. Forget it."

I was thinking about that woman dragged from the bus. I could never tell them about her, but I thought about her all the time. Maybe she'd dressed up that day. Maybe she'd decided to wear that skirt, the green one, the knee-length one, and found the shoes to match. She'd fixed her hair and fed him his breakfast, her baby, with his eyelashes that curled up to the sky. She'd probably assumed the day would be like any other day, when she'd hoped for a few moments of contentment: a friendly glance in her direction, a feeling of doing something decent and good, an ice cream or a sunset.

It seems people who understand you the most are the ones most capable of destroying you.

"I think it's good to ask questions about people," Esteban said. "Especially nowadays, it's smart to know which side people are on. My uncle has had some problems in his café, he'd hired some Bolshevik without knowing it."

"No, that's not why I—"

Suddenly a burst of guitar strings rang out from inside the house, one of those swelling, patriotic tunes, and Martín said we should take the guitar and play some Spinetta. He put his cigarette between his lips and screwed up his face as his hands ran up and down an invisible guitar.

I asked Esteban where his cigarettes came from. Esteban said he didn't know.

"What's with you lately, man? Are you messing with commies? Look at fucking Che Guevara over here!" Martín said.

"I'm not a commie," I said. Then I wished I hadn't. I tried smoking to change the subject, to get the aftertaste of the word, and all it implied to my friends, out of my mouth. I had trouble pulling out the cigarette from the packet—I couldn't get my thumb and finger around the thin stem. When I finally birthed the crooked stick, I ran it under my nose, feeling the skin smooth between my fingers. It was so light.

Padre Pedro appeared at the entry of the patio, and coughed gently. I wondered how long he'd been listening. Martín looked at us and put his glass of whisky behind his chair.

"Padre Pedro, do you know your constellations?" he called out. He was smooth, Martín.

"Most of them, yes," said Padre Pedro, strolling in our direction.

"There's the Southern Cross," he said, folding his hands across his stomach, just beneath his own personal crucifix, which dangled from his neck. As he stood there in his cassock, looking at the sky, I realized he wasn't very old. He had a round face and round glasses to match. I found it amazing that he would choose not to be with a woman, or man, or whatever.

Utter loneliness.

"I have always wanted to paint the night sky. I would paint different shades of black on a canvas. No one ever thinks of that, do they?"

Padre Pedro's hands unfolded across the sky.

Martín agreed that would be interesting.

"Yes. It would be an exercise in humility. Sometimes we have to think about the universe, to remember our own place in this world, no?" Padre Pedro said.

We nodded. Padre Pedro looked back at the stars.

"We need to take time to reflect, to think about the darkness and the light, and decide on which side we fall. Our Creator moves us to the light, but we need to be open to Him."

We continued nodding, as though we'd been talking about that when he arrived. Then he began to pace from the shrub on one side to the strange mermaid statue on the other.

"Sometimes, boys, in our lives, we forget to honour those who are most important. We become enamored of rock stars, fashion, and long hair. We look to a lifestyle that is a precursor to sin, and darkness."

I didn't know how to say that I disagreed. We all want to reach for transcendence, for a purpose, but life is on earth. We only long for meaning because otherwise we're born and we disappear for no reason at all and that hurts our egos.

Padre Pedro had his back to us, and Martín started running his hands up and down again, like Spinetta playing guitar.

After that we decided to go out. Padre Pedro was creeping us out, and I felt like looking at the ocean. When we said goodbye to Martín's mother, she said, "Don't forget to pay attention to your dreams—a dream is a body's most honest communication with itself."

She's so strange.

The bars were mostly empty. It was still early. We found a place with a pool table, and Martín ordered some drinks. When he returned, though, he asked me how it was going in the slums.

"What are you talking about?" I asked.

"Mariana told me. She knows about your trip with Bárbara. She said you two are chummy with some dangerous people."

"What the fuck, Martín? Who are you to talk about me behind my—"

"You're lucky I didn't say anything at my house. If the wrong person had heard?" He shook his head. I was dumbstruck, and I knew I was inviting ridicule when I told him they were some of the nicest people I've ever met, and not at all dangerous.

"*Sos un pelotudo,*" he told me, and Esteban nodded in agreement.

I told him he didn't know what he was talking about. He told me I didn't know what I was getting into. He called Bárbara a Commie bitch, so I left.

He didn't know what it was like to have this feeling, to feel that a person has crawled out of the earth for you, their bones and parts all joined together by red clay and black mud—all for you. The pull in your chest tells you. It's burning and drowning and dreaming and longing and a slow fade into darkness.

Outside, there was a warm wind and I blinked in the bright night as I waited at the street for the cars to pass. The breeze brought a feeling of being followed. I turned to my left, where a couple was eating ice cream. They were laughing because the girl's long hair kept whipping into her mouth. I thought of Bárbara and the taste of her skin, but then turned back to look into the eye of a rifle.

"Identity documents?"

A man in a dark suit. Two other men behind him. They were clean-shaven and handsome. I told him I didn't have the documents, so he walked behind me, slowly, the rifle caressing my skin in a slow semicircle until it reached my back, where it bore down. At that moment I saw an airplane on the horizon, tracing the border between sea and sky.

"*Mi pana*. Why don't you have your papers?"

He said it so softly, almost like a lover, into my ear.

I told him I didn't know we had to have them. That was a lie, of course. He told me I'd need to come with them, then. He grabbed my arm.

I panicked, until I saw Esteban and Martín rushing up to us, their eyes round in alarm. Martín told the man holding me that his father is an admiral, and he would give him a call if this went any further. Martín can be an asshole but at least he's loyal.

The men asked his name, then looked at each other and the one holding me loosened his grip. They let me go. But not before telling me to get a fucking haircut.

The weather was edging its way towards a storm and my *abuelita* started twitching around the house, aching to get out, like a cat who feels atmospheric pressure she suspected the world would soon compress and release, and she craved the transition and change. It drove her wild. As soon as the rain began, always sudden, usually unexpected by the rest of us, she dashed out to drive through the storm. She forced me to go with her and I never had the heart to tell her that the lightning was like black stars behind my skull, the thunder a swelling of my skull.

Bárbara came to get me because we needed to help Kiki and Carlos in the shantytown. We hadn't seen them since the wedding and we wanted to feel safe. We were comforted by their clean, colourful house and their hot, rich food. Not to mention their silly jokes and lack of fear. They'd already suffered, and had nothing left to lose.

At the bus stop, birds flew overhead in V-formation, gliding across the expanse, creating shadows of blue and grey. They'd undoubtedly come from the north, pulled by magnets, charting their way to the bottom of the world.

When we arrived at the pile of rubble where the shantytown had been, Bárbara cried. I hurt my foot by kicking a fucking rock. A three-legged dog waltzed past us. One lone wire hung between two trees—white laundry blowing in the wind against a blue sky, like the froth and spray of the ocean.

Like a flag of surrender.

I woke up with a throbbing foot and head. My mother bent over the newspaper, which was spread on the table next to her toast. She read the article written by the Housing Commission out loud: "Our only intention is that those who live in our city be culturally prepared for it. To live in this city isn't just for everyone, just for those who deserve it ..."

Even my *abuelita* was silent.

I had to attend another of Bárbara's meetings. It had become personal. I started out on foot, wending my way along a nautical knot through the city in case I was being followed. I hadn't seen Bárbara since the day we'd visited the ruins of the shantytown. We'd sat on the rubble until a man yelled at us to leave. Afterwards, Bárbara had been afraid. So had I.

The building was surrounded by a cheap wire fence and had a rickety fire escape littered with garbage. I entered the building and stood in the doorway while my eyes adjusted to the dark. I hardly recognized my own shadow, where the sun rushed in from behind. In the half-light, the wall slowly took shape and solidified, like paint spreading over a canvas. Or blood spilling across the floor.

Posters of various sizes and colours announced concerts and poetry readings. One particular notice of a naked woman advertised an art exhibition that was supposed to have taken place a year ago. Her breasts had been covered by paint. I thought it was kind that someone protected her modesty.

I passed through a glass door and made my way down a long, dark corridor, moving in the direction of the low hum of voices. When I found them, they were in a jagged semicircle, listening to a man who paced up and down one side of the room.

I stood in the doorway, hidden from view. I scanned the room, which was normally reserved as a practice space for rock bands, but rock music was evaporating so the room was free for other purposes. An older man with a thick moustache and a heavy wool sweater sat on an amplifier, and a small woman with big hair like Mario Kempes was cross-legged at the drums. I spotted Bárbara at the back of the room, her head bowed over her notepad as she scribbled the instructions of the pacing man. A rose among thorns.

He was tall, with dark-rimmed glasses and his hair parted almost completely. He was visibly agitated, this man who seemed more university professor than revolutionary, and his voice rose with every sentence he uttered—sentences that escaped from him like birds, with angry words like manifesto and sentiment, government and detention. A demure woman sitting on the side of the group made small worried noises and placed her arm horizontally, pushing the air downwards, insisting that he lower his volume.

The man paid no attention to her but stopped talking to take a sip of water. As he did so, I sidled into the room and waited awkwardly. Everyone looked at me except for Bárbara, who was still writing in her notepad. I smiled at the expectant, defiant eyes, reaching for my cigarettes in my back pocket. Everyone tensed then, shoulders raised in unison.

"It's all right, I invited him," Bárbara said, matter-of-factly and to no one in particular. I nodded at her and she smiled back.

Then she mouthed the words: *te amo.*

I took a seat next to Bárbara and held her free hand. I listened as they discussed the ban on public demonstrations, on labour movement and trade union activity. They talked about censorship of fashion, free love, and divorce. They read the names of the students who had been beaten. They didn't need to mention the increasingly frequent disappearances of colleagues, friends, and family. I knew Bárbara was thinking about the destruction of the shantytowns.

The city had turned into a house of horrors.

They discussed the importance of supplying their organizations with money, arms, and medical supplies, in order to distribute the goods among the poor. They spoke about the gangs formed for abductions and how they operated in green Ford Falcons, kidnapping people and ransacking homes. They spoke about clandestine centers for prolonged detention.

"My sister was abducted. Her name was only written in the address book of a friend, who happened to be a lawyer representing a political prisoner," the man sitting on the amplifier said.

"My cousin was taken for her involvement in a social protest over school bus fares," said another woman.

The professor spoke. "No one is safe. People are paralyzed by indifference, ignorance, or fear."

Then he handed out a paper.

Por cada obrero secuestrado, un patrón y un milico reventado.

My head swam and the voices reached me like radio waves, distant and filtered as though through water. I began to draw so I could drown them out. Strained voices coming from the depths were interrupted by other, clearer voices, repeating the words spoken but altering their meaning, so that what was said was suddenly imbued with a purpose that I could finally understand. I knew now why I was involved, and what I had to do.

I might have been a writer whose story had already been written. I felt inspired in my head, but I didn't have time to get my words down. Well, time was not really the problem. It's more that the thoughts were not concrete; they were abstract. Concepts. Images. That's why I drew, instead of writing. Symbols are easier to translate, interpret, and understand. For some reason, it was all I could manage.

I also thought they were less likely to incriminate.

Bárbara and I left the brown brick building separately after kissing in the darkened hallway.

"You give me strength," she said.

Her words came from somewhere else, and it was like watching someone else's life from above. This boy told her that he loved her. He kissed this girl, loved her truly. He kissed her again then walked to Martín's house.

I floated down the street, my heart a big red balloon. Then I went inside without knocking and found Martín's mother, Graciela, sitting on the couch reading a book. She immediately stood up to kiss me, as though she had been expecting me. Her high-heeled shoes made her taller, so that I was at the height of her fragrant neck. I asked if Martín was around.

"I think he's in his room. How are you, Andrés?" she asked, her accent odd, pronouncing the "r" not with her tongue but with her lips and throat.

I admitted that I wasn't feeling very good. That things were a little crazy right now. That everything felt tense.

"Yes, things are tense—for good cause, though. Once things get back to normal, we'll be able to relax again, no?" She cocked her head, an amused smile on her face, and caressed my shoulder.

The floor shifted and I lost my balance. I laughed, stepping backwards.

"I think I'll go find Martín now."

Graciela said nothing, and sat back down with her book, perched on the edge of her cream-coloured couch.

When I knocked on Martín's door, there was no answer. I opened the door a crack and peered in, finding Martín asleep on his bed, face down. He was still wearing his clothes and hadn't taken off his shoes. His mouth was open, and there was a dark stain on his pillow. His room hadn't changed much in the years I had known him—the light blue walls and model airplanes were still there as they had been ten years before.

He had new books now, though. If I'd been the writer, then Martín was the reader. He devoured books at an astronomical pace and seemed to be able to quote authors at the drop of a hat. Only his good friends knew that about him, though I wasn't sure I was a good friend anymore.

I sat down at Martín's desk, waiting for him to wake up. I lit a cigarette and swung around on the chair. Martín's impeccable cadet uniforms hung in the closet and his boots were lined up underneath. There were three pairs, two of which were perfectly shiny. One pair was caked in mud. Martín stirred, breathed in and out. His exhalation sounded wet. Then he opened his eyes, rubbed his mouth with the back of his arm and rolled onto his back.

"*¿Puta, Andrés, qué haces aquí?*" he asked, eyes squinting and mouth turned down.

"Can't I visit my friend when I feel like it?"

"Not when you wake me up, *concha de tu hermana*. Christ, I barely got any sleep last night."

I took a drag of my cigarette and watched my friend rub his face, then head over to the toilet. He didn't close the door. His urine was fast and hard against the ceramic.

"What were you doing all night?" I finally asked.

"Just busy now," he said from the bathroom. On his way back into the room, he opened his bedroom door and shouted for someone to bring two coffees.

"Were you with Mariana?" I asked.

"No, I wish. I've been doing some work for my dad. That's all."

"What do you mean? Like those assholes who stopped us?"

"They stopped you, *pelotudo*. And they let you go thanks to my dad, so a little gratitude might be in order."

"Martín, what kind of work are you doing?"

"Reconnaissance, mostly," he answered, sitting down on his bed. "I have to do my part."

"Reconnaissance?"

"For subversives."

Martín put his foot up on the chair where I was sitting, and leaned over with his nail clippers. With a cigarette hanging over his bottom lip, he proceeded to cut his toenails. A knock at the door, and the servant with black hair entered and placed two coffee cups on Martín's desk. He nodded at me, took his silver tray and left.

"Martín, should I be worried?"

"Do you have anything to be worried about?" Martín continued to cut his nails, a small smile at the corner of his mouth. I brushed a toenail off my lap. "You've always been too soft. My friend, as a great man once said—all within the state, nothing outside the state, nothing against the state. That's all."

"What?"

"Don't worry about it. It'll all be over soon, my friend. Even failure can move the needle towards justice. *La puta que me parió,* I've cut my nail too short—fucking nail clippers."

How to live now? If one has resources, those questions are multiplied and possibilities endless; I had some resources, some options and only one dream: to write and live with Bárbara. I had never considered another life, until the opportunity for sacrifice was presented to me. She was willing to do it, of course. I thought we would just be feeding people, but eventually it became more serious and I was asked to partake in activities that might lead to my imminent demise. Or hers. What could I do?

Martín came looking for me today. He rang the doorbell, but I told my *abuelita* to lie and say I was out. I am scared of him now. What did he mean when he said "even failure can move the needle towards justice?" I listened to them talk.

Martín's usually nervous around my *abuelita* because she's proud of who she is, urban working class, and doesn't take any shit. Once she read his palm and said he was destined for some kind of purgatory.

"Martín, you look like shit, *mijito.*"

"I know. But you look lovely, Doña Josefa. I like your hair."

I could picture my *abuelita* touching her purple-tinted hair, raising her painted brow.

"You're looking for Andrés."

"Well, yes, I mean, I was originally. But now I see you, I think I've changed my mind."

I could picture Martín too, leaning against the door frame, thinking he was so charming.

"In that case, why don't you come in? Andrés and Marta are

out, we could have us some fun."

By now I bet she was untying her apron strings. My abuelita is the best.

"I just meant that you look lovely ..." he said quickly.

"*Baboso*. You think I want to bang around with a little stick like you? Forget it!"

As he turned to go, he must have looked at the phone. If he had, and if he had squinted, he would have seen the paper next to it, where I'd written *Plaza - 16h30. Bring bottles.*

Bárbara and I had planned to go to the plaza with her group. The square (actually an oval) was often host to puppet shows, theatrical events, and other spectacles. When we arrived, the area was relatively clear of festivities. Twenty or so people were milling around, men and women, some our age but most a bit older.

Most held maté gourds or Thermoses of coffee. In a corner, a couple of men opened boxes. Women walked around carrying piles of paper, cigarettes dangling from their mouths.

The air felt warm and heavy, full of water, though something smelled like petrol. Everyone seemed focused, driven, but suddenly, I couldn't move my limbs.

A tall man dressed all in black raised his arm. They lifted bottles and someone held a flame. Women turned their heads, lifted their shoulders. I was rooted to the ground. It occurred to me then that all we want is access to someone's brain—to float in their synapses, to make them laugh and lust. That is memory, that is love. The notes of understanding that pass between us all are invisible and silent, a persuasive percussion.

Molotov cocktails. Explosives. Bárbara called my name. I wasn't going to purgatory with Martín, I was going to hell. Another shout: bottles crashing, explosions, flames.

I saw Martín's face through the smoke.

We all retreated to a café as far from the Plazoleta as we could get. One of the bottles had broken, and cut the legs of an older woman walking on the street. Martín had been taken to the hospital, he had fallen to the ground with his arm covering his eyes.

He was screaming about his eyes. Something had happened to his eyes.

I walk to the hospital. Esteban is just leaving after visiting with Martín, but he pulls me aside, grabs my arm, and tells me to be careful. I don't ask him why I would need to be careful—that is my first mistake. Martín lies in bed, with yellow bandages covering his eyes. I sit next to him for a while and just watch. His chest rises and falls. I never realized how relaxing it is to watch someone in a deep sleep. When a nurse enters the room, she tells me she has to change his bandages, and that I might not want to watch. She leaves and his breathing changes. He has woken up. He knows I'm there.

"Andrés, you have to hide me," he says.

His mouth is slack and moves like a marionette, as though he's a puppet and made of wood. He says he needs help. He says his father is furious about the meeting, the explosion, and the accident.

"But we didn't force you to come with us. You followed us," I said.

He said his father still blames us. He said his father doesn't mess around. He said his father never wants to see him again.

He asks me again to hide him.

I tell Martín to hide at Bárbara's house, where she lives with the others. I even tell him where he can find it. This is my second mistake.

Bárbara's place is a half hour away on foot. The main house is huge and dirty. It looks empty, though I'm not sure whether it is. Through the shrubs on the side of the house I can see the small window of the shed, like a reflective, unblinking eye. I imagine Juan Pablo standing at the window watching for me. He answers the door, wearing combat boots, and tells me she's gone. I can see the other roommates standing behind him, shooting glances my way. They pace and smoke. He shuts the door in my face. What will he do when Martín arrives? I consider whether I should warn him. This is my third mistake.

I walk through the park where I had eaten with Bárbara just a few weeks ago, when my mind was clear. Despite sunshine, a fog seeps through my thoughts. I have to walk carefully in the rose garden. It is full of scents, sounds, and memory, almost overwhelming. The manicured plants and bushes hiding the interior chaos—the amoral, inexplicable quality of nature. The pebbles enter my shoes and pierce my feet. A bird lands on a branch in front of me. I don't know what kind of bird it is, but I think it is a sign of hope or redemption. The flitting, fickle bird does not indulge me and flies off into the sky, leaving me to continue on my way, trying to avoid the thorns.

For those living in the enormous city, the darkness relieved them of their daytime responsibilities so that they could give themselves over to the caprices of the night. For many, it brought relief, as thoughts turned from work to food, drink, music and touch. For me, electric lights and human noise were no match for the imposing presence of the dark. It descended on my shoulders like the burden of my culpability. I stood on the boardwalk, looking at the ocean that was turning black and silent. It seemed to be biding its time, as unpredictable as any person. Waiting.

I would not take the bus anymore and had lost weight as a result. My large frightened eyes, my thin countenance and—despite the warning against it—my long hair, convinced people to keep their distance as I walked determinedly away from the ocean. Like *el extraño del pelo largo*. No one looked me in the eye. No one looked at anything, they all seemed too busy, rushing through their lives like shadows. I had in fact been walking for weeks, trying to avoid green Ford Falcons, watching the ocean and the cemeteries, wondering if my answer to Martín's plea had in fact set in motion a series of events that would lead to Bárbara's death.

I am writing in the present tense, to provide assurances that love will be preserved, and those we care about will not disappear.

I wonder if a secret can kill you, if you don't give it away?

When I arrive at her mother's apartment, I press the buzzer at the door of the building. There is a crackle and a sound like a cough, and her mother, whom I had never met, answers in a husky voice.

"Buenas tardes, Doña Liria, soy Andrés," I say.

After a moment, she buzzes me in. When I step out of the elevator onto the sixth floor, I can see that Bárbara's door is ajar—the space filled by her mother. I lean in to give a customary kiss on the cheek, but she makes no effort to kiss me back. She stands still, smelling of onions and cigarettes. Even though Bárbara is adopted, her mother's face and body somehow resemble Bárbara's, though her hair is lighter and wavier.

"So you're Andrés," she says.

I nod and smile, but Liria just stands there. I wonder if she will let me in the house. She finally turns with a tired wave of her hand. As I walk through the small apartment, I look for Bárbara on the brown couch or upholstered chairs. She is not there. When we pass her mother's bedroom I look in with a rush of excitement and guilt over all the times we'd made love on the large, silky bed.

Bárbara had never taken me into her own bedroom, and I had never asked to see it. Liria stops in the doorway and asks me to stay put. I peek into the room, painted a pale grey-pink colour. There is an old-fashioned white dresser and a large mirror with some wooden jewelry dangling off of it, which I recognize as Bárbara's favourite necklaces. I am surprised to see her in bed. Liria walks up to her quietly and delicately shakes her shoulder. I keep a respectful distance as Liria whispers something in Bárbara's ear. As she leaves the room, she affords me a small, serious nod.

I approach Bárbara slowly. Her silky, straight hair is spread out and her pillow has engraved lines in her cheek, reminding me of a mosaic pattern. I sit on her bed, relieved to rest my tired legs, and she removes her arm to reveal puffy, red eyes. A look of alarm crosses her face—wind blowing across long grass.

"Are you all right?"

"I just wanted to see you," I say, reaching out to caress her cheek. She closes her eyes and breathes in deeply. There are tissues on her bedside table and a red plastic bucket on the floor.

"*¿Estás bien?*" I ask.

She opens her eyes, and looks at me suddenly and with fear. "Andrés, you should ask yourself that question."

"What do you mean?"

"You haven't called me in weeks."

"What?"

"You haven't called, or come by. I've been worried. I went to see your mother the other day, and she didn't know where you

169

were either. Mariana said that someone from school had seen you out by the ocean."

"That's just not true. I saw you just the other day, at your meeting."

She raises herself on her elbows. Her freckles seem darker as her skin is so pale.

Quietly she says, "That was two weeks ago."

She takes my hand softly in her own, rubbing it with her thumb. "There's one other thing I need to ask you," she says. "Do you remember talking to Martín?"

I think I might need to use her bucket myself.

"Bárbara, did he do something?"

She looks down at her lap. She shakes her head.

"He's blind now. You remember? But he didn't do anything, *mi amor.* You did."

When I left Bárbara's apartment, the night was fully unveiled, exposing itself in all its splendour. I stood outside for a moment, looking at a shiny gum wrapper on the ground. Could it have been two weeks? I searched for a cigarette, knowing that it would only make me more nauseous. The kiss that Bárbara had given me after the meeting was still fresh in my memory. She had tasted like the ocean. Had she been crying? When was that? A voice called behind me, a deep male voice. I turned and saw them, waiting for me. The men with the greased hair, shinier for the streetlight. There were three of them, leaning on their dark green car, casually smoking cigarettes. I ran. I ran from them through the city, past conjoined houses of various sunset shades of orange, peach, and red, until I made it to my maroon-coloured door. When I opened it, my grandmother and mother were huddled together at the kitchen table. My grandmother's eyeshadow was smudged across her forehead.

The yellow kitchen telephone was on the table in front of them. My mother's eyes widened when I entered, then they filled with tears.

"Where were you?" she gasped.

"I don't know," I answered, and rushed into my room. I packed my bag, bringing enough clothes for both myself and for Bárbara, and some extra in case Martín and Esteban needed them too. My ashtray had been moved, as had my book. I heard men's voices outside my window, whispering and laughing. My mother came into my room when she heard me screaming out the empty window. She glanced at my bag and hugged me. Suggested I should shower and eat, as I was going away.

By writing about her so much, I fear I may have taken something away from her person. Rather than immortalize her, I have killed her.

PART IV

HALF-LIGHT

Chapter 12

Jana drags Tess to a party. Their feet slip on wet cobblestone streets as they pass tourist shops, galleries that look like warehouses on the outside, and narrow, trendy brunch places.

"Marcos once brought me to that spa over there, the one that looks like shipping containers out there in the water. It was fun."

Tess nods, lost in thought.

"We could go sometime," she says, smiling at Tess. "Or maybe you'll meet someone at this party—"

"I invited Olivier."

"You did? Don't get me wrong, I like Olivier, but he's so ... opinionated. You need someone—"

"Jana, what happens when you're stuck in someone else's story?"

"What do you mean?"

"I mean, when you mistake their story for your own, and you can't move away, or move on?"

Jana doesn't miss a beat.

"Scheherazade saved her own life with stories."

"Yes, but I want to save someone else."

They arrive at the party in an elegant, lofty apartment overlooking the river. The owner of the apartment is a friend of the guys they met at the café, a painter named Marcel, who is all eyelashes and jaw—not to mention tall, svelte, and well-dressed. He has decorated his apartment in a nautical theme, explaining in his rolling Arabic accent that he comes from a family of shipowners.

Jana sparkles around the room, pulling Tess with her, introducing herself to everyone. She's so good at this. When confronted with someone she doesn't know, Jana asks them questions about their professions and hobbies. No one minds. Her enthusiasm is open and genuine and she pulls them in.

When it's Tess's turn to introduce herself, Jana jumps in, calls her "the sweetest roommate in the world," and tells people she's a social worker. Tess doesn't correct her.

The room is packed with accomplished, attractive, young people: the director of a human rights organization, a symphony conductor, a therapist, a painter. Tess feels anxiety wash over her, pebbles and sand rubbing her skin. She hopes Olivier arrives soon, so she has someone to talk to. She can't talk to strangers. She picks the sticker off her beer bottle and rolls it into a little ball. Jana leaves to smoke a cigarette on the balcony. Tess can see her profile against the twilit sky. It's a beautiful night, and the air is still warm enough to open the windows and patio doors. The water of the river reflects a sliver of moon.

She stands next to the hors d'oeuvres because she doesn't know where else to go. She bobs her head to the music, just enough, and decides to switch to wine. This is a fancy party. The ambient music fills the room, soars above the clouds. She thought she'd be overdressed in the outfit Jana picked out for her. She wears a navy-blue jumpsuit with a beaded necklace. Jana had curled her hair and applied her makeup, complimenting Tess the entire time on her beautiful golden eyes, her clear skin and silky hair.

Tess had loved being close enough to Jana that she could smell her.

She reminds herself to pace her drinks.

A man approaches her and she tenses. He wears a familiar newsboy cap and cord slacks. She can't remember where she's seen him before, but she's drawn to him. He tells her in about thirty seconds that he grew up in Paris with a white French mother and a Black American father. He is a professor, but doesn't know many people in the city yet. Tess figured he'd honed his elevator pitch in networking events and parties because it was good—rehearsed. He didn't have to think too much. Or maybe he was sick of being asked where he was from.

His eyes are dark and bright. Not to mention his accent—subtle yet present, like her sex drive. Still, she would rather not have to flirt right now. She was perfectly happy standing on her own.

His name is Antoine.

"Call me Tony," he says, and smiles—dimples kissing his cheeks. "But we've met before, no? Marie, right?"

The man who approached her at the park. Why does he keep reappearing in her life, searching for this elusive Marie?

"No, no. My name is Tess." She releases an awkward laugh.

"Tony and Tess. Has a nice ring to it, *non*?"

Tess smiles and nods, feels her face flush as she grabs some veggies and dip. She's not used to such confidence. She's angered by the fact that his attentions feel good. She thinks for a brief moment of Cam, and then of Olivier, and feels a brief, momentary shudder of guilt.

Where is Olivier?

"What do you teach, Tony?"

"History and political science mostly."

"Oh."

She doesn't have a follow-up question, and panics. She has three choices: she can remain silent; she can act like a silly little woman who wants to learn from a man; or she can formulate an intelligent question.

An intelligent question could result in his thinking she wants to impress him.

He's probably used to it—he must have so many students falling for him, crushing on him, throwing themselves at him.

Tony is smooth.

"And what do you do, Tess?"

"Well, not much yet. I'm a social worker, but I just moved here. I'm doing some volunteer stuff for now."

"Oh?"

"With me," Olivier sidles up beside her, beer in hand. He doesn't touch her in a particularly possessive way, he just nudges her arm with his elbow as he smiles his beautiful smile, but Tony takes a step backward.

"Oh, this is Olivier," she smiles at Tony.

"Glad you could make it. Excuse me for one moment, please."

She leaves them together and heads to the restroom. Olivier didn't dress up and looks shabby next to Tony. She likes that he doesn't conform or feel the need to give in to social conventions, but at the same time she's put off. He has the luxury of not having to impress anyone. He doesn't need to care what anyone thinks. He can simply show up and smile.

She feels guilty for leaving them together, but she's confident they can find something to talk about. She's not responsible for them, and she doesn't think she can handle the pressure right now of standing next to two beautiful, intelligent people who think she's someone else. Jana must have made her look really good when she did her makeup. She doesn't want to disappoint. As she looks for the bathroom, she glances at a television screen in Marcel's bedroom, where someone is flipping through channels on a flatscreen TV.

She admires the bathroom as she finishes her wine in front of the mirror. The blue and white decorations, the pretty towels, the scented soaps and tiny vases make her think of a luxury hotel in the Mediterranean. She wishes she could go to one.

She returns to the living room to refill her wine, but doesn't see Jana. She only sees Tony and Olivier talking, but she can't go back to them just yet. She decides to sneak into the TV room. At least she won't have to speak.

She slides in and stands pressed against a wall. The room is now full of men and buzzing with expectation, and out of the corner of her eye, she spots Jana's shiny bare shoulder.

"The category, Government and Politics. Clue, for $600: he used the expression 'rugged individualism' when running for president in 1928."

"Who is Herbert Hoover?"

Jana answers before any of the contestants on Jeopardy. The men all cheer for her. She looks gorgeous and confident, the blue of the TV reflected in her smiling eyes.

"The category, Recent World History. Clue, for $800: a state terror network joining military dictatorships from Ecuador to Argentina." Everyone in the room looks at Jana.

"What is Operation Condor?"

She knew the answer again. She nods and bows to the people clapping around her, then focuses again on the screen.

Tess sidles up to her, feeling proud of her friend.

"Jana, you're brilliant! Can I ask you later about your last answer? Please don't let me forget."

"Sure, let's go. I'm creaming these guys, and don't want them to feel bad," she says in a loud voice, as she stands to take her leave.

The guys all laugh.

"She got five correct in a row!" Hari says, and eyes linger on Jana as she walks past.

They head to the living room, where Olivier and Tony are engaged in a conversation. Their voices are loud. They stand just next to the table of snacks and drinks. There are no non-alcoholic options, Tess notes, so she has no choice but to drink. There is a cheese plate and vegetable tray. Jana fills both their glasses with red wine, says a quick hello to Olivier and remains standing close to the men. They're speaking in French, and Tess realizes they're having a discussion about the Internet.

She catches snippets of their conversation as she interrogates Jana.

"So you want to know about Operation Condor? It started in the mid seventies, encouraged by the US. A Cold War thing. To prevent the spread of armed revolution across South America," Jana says.

"Don't want to miss out, yet don't want to commit. Want to be in the world and apart at the same time," Olivier is saying.

Tess drinks her Shiraz.

"Tens of thousands of people were 'disappeared' during the '70s and '80s. All these governments were sending death squads to one another's territories. It's taken decades to figure out what happened. People weren't tried or convicted of anything. Just kidnapped, tortured, and murdered. But you learned about this, right?" Jana asks Tess.

"Mmhm. Of course. I do wonder though about those who disappeared. Have the people responsible been brought to justice?"

Tess feels an unbearable helplessness. A hypocrisy. Here they are standing around, drinking wine, hoping to get laid, while discussing people's pain. She'd been in many of these situations—mostly people trying to prove they're the most knowledgeable, the most compassionate, without realizing they're capitalizing on people's anguish. Trying to be interesting, trying to seem informed, trying to shock and entertain.

She had no idea a network like that could have covered so many countries. Where had Mr. Hewitt lived? Should he be brought to justice? Why was he so elusive about it?

She hears Tony. *"Yes, but don't you think there's an argument to be made that social media and the Internet could actually preserve human intimacy, rather than dissolving it?"*

Jana winks at Hari who has walked by, and continues speaking.

"No, you're absolutely right. It hasn't been forgotten, but it's complex. Think of all the national laws, international treaties and rulings by human rights tribunals that have to be considered. There are people, you know, survivors, family members, lawyers, who are working on it, but it's slow. So much damage can be done in no time at all, but piecing it out takes so much longer."

Tess wonders where Mr. Hewitt fits into this. As a romantic poet volunteering in soup kitchens, she would guess he was one of the good guys. But he seemed to have a number of influences, not least of which was Martín.

Olivier's voice is so loud.

"How in the world could it be its preservation? It's saturated with so much bullshit, any genuine feeling is obscured or satirized. The "cloud" is now our collective consciousness, and it saps all meaning from life like ... vapour from air," Olivier says.

"And the US wanted to strengthen anti-communist forces, so they pumped weapons and money into the region," Jana says.

"But we're searching for connection. You said it's now a collective consciousness. Isn't that a good thing? Think about how it

has revolutionized the way we share information and organize ourselves. Every act, whether of love or aggression, can now be recorded and shared with the world," Tony says.

"They ended up with torture camps and crematoriums," Jana says.

"But where's the oversight? It can be controlled and propaganda is the result. And instead of connection, it polarizes. It's echo chambers that do nothing but make us feel vindicated by feeding us our own beliefs," Olivier answers.

Everyone hears Olivier and all the conversation in the room pauses. He looks around and continues.

"It lets people get away with apathy. They think it's enough to re-post something on social media. So many crises today, and with the exception of those who have no choice but to confront their reality, people turn the other way. No one takes any real action on behalf of anyone else."

"It seems we're all angry," Jana says. She eats a baby carrot. Tony and Olivier seem to have come to a truce.

"But that's just it, isn't it?" Tess says. "People in these countries, they knew something awful was going down, but unless they were exceptionally brave they would have looked the other way, right?"

The men seem excited now to contribute to the women's conversation.

Tony actually cuts in. Tess is shamefully relieved that he switches to English.

"You were talking about dictatorships in the '70s and '80s? Yes, well, the propaganda was fierce." He looks at Olivier. "But some of the revolutionary groups were dangerous, too. Some of them set cars on fire, planted explosives in hotels, killed policemen, things like that. No denying the repression against them was intense. Many people disappeared who weren't even connected to the armed groups. It was horrendous."

"How do you both know this?" Tess asks.

"I research and teach history," Tony answers.

"I know because of Marcos ... you know, Mr. García. His parents," Jana answers.

"I read," Olivier says.

"I bet you read the Internet!" Tony laughs.

Tess refills her glass.

"I don't want to ask, but how did people disappear?"

Tony answers. "It depends. In some cases they were buried in the desert, or their bodies were burned, or they were drugged, stripped, and loaded onto planes to be tossed into the ocean. In almost all cases they wanted to hide the bodies."

She watches his mouth form words that seem so sharp, like steel. She feels sick to her stomach. She is certain Bárbara ended up in the ocean. She takes a gulp of her wine. She tries to round out her own words, make them soft.

"What did people do about this?"

She meant it in a rhetorical manner but he answers her. Taking her cue, he also speaks gently.

"People were afraid. They reasoned that if people were being detained, they must have done something to 'deserve' it."

"But relatives? People who knew them? What about Marcos and his family?"

Jana answers this one.

"Governments were powerful and twisted the truth, exaggerated the threat, making people question their own realities. And of course, tons of people were either indifferent or ignorant of what was happening. There's a lot of guilt in Marcos's family. But many are still searching. They haven't given up."

Tess sips her wine slowly and tries not to look at the others too closely. She feels her mind roll over like a wave. She's unsure how to continue this conversation. She realizes she hasn't introduced Jana and Tony. She doesn't care. She has an urge for pizza or poutine. Some comfort food. She wants to tell Jana to meet her on the balcony. She wants to pay attention to the dark blue of the sky. She wants to look at the river, the ribbon carving its way out to sea.

She wants someone to hold her. Tony keeps talking.

"Almost everyone was in the dark. They had no idea these dictatorships were so cruel. Also, until bodies were found, they held onto hope that their kids might be alive. Perhaps not knowing is harder than knowing."

"I wonder what I would do in a situation like that. Don't you? Would you respond with courage? Would you know to do what is right?" Tess asks.

Olivier answers.

"It happens all over. Here too. It's different, but it's the same. Violence is everywhere. Are you doing what's right?"

"What is right?" Tess asks.

"Checking on your neighbours," Olivier answers.

In the restroom, Tess chugs another glass of wine and thinks about those who disappeared, and the double-edged sword of not knowing. The nightmare left to the family members. How would they imagine their loved ones' final moments? Or would they be forever shackled to a tiny hope?

Tess's mother's final exhalation still haunts her. She witnessed it in the hospital room and, at the time, wished her mother could have explained what she was experiencing. Still, Tess was there with her and was able to invent her own interpretation. She knew her mother was safe, and she was afforded the luxury of imagining a kind exit. The worst purgatory would be that of the family members waiting, wondering, wishing. How easy it would be to give up, which would feel like a betrayal.

When she returns to the living room, she sees that Jana is on the balcony talking to Hari, and Olivier is nowhere to be seen. Probably outside smoking a joint. Tony is waiting for her, and has poured another glass of wine. For her.

Another one.

"Are you writing a paper or article about this? I can send you some information," he says.

"That's nice of you, thank you. I'm just curious for personal reasons."

"Oh?"

"I can't really talk about it, but I really appreciate your help." She has a hard time forming her words.

"Does this have to do with a boyfriend?" he smiles. She's annoyed at his sheepish pretense, and the fact that he's cute. Despite herself, she looks again for Olivier. She's not there to flirt with anyone, even if she's wearing her hair down. This is serious.

"No, not a boyfriend."

"And Olivier's not ..."

"Uh, no. He's not," she says. Her thoughts swim. She's definitely tipsy. "But it is someone that I love," she adds.

Tony nods. "Why don't I give you my number? You can call me any time you have a question."

She accepts Tony's number. She also accepts his offer to walk her home. Despite her annoyance, she accepts his offer to sleep in her bed. She's not sure why she's done this, except that it's probably healthier than going home to scroll through messages from Cam, or wondering what happened to Olivier, or drinking herself into oblivion.

Chapter 13

Winter first warns of its arrival with a whisper. When it hits town, no one is prepared. From one day to the next, a frosted cloak descends on the city. The city struggles to maintain its rhythm and sensuality while people dig out their parkas and toques from their closets. When Tess walks outside, the brutal wind makes mirrors of her eyes and the city cracks under the cold.

A time for introspection and hunkering down. Yet there's always light, even if just reflections glancing off snow, and only for a few hours of the day. There is beauty. The skies, at dusk, take on a texture like pastel-coloured silk—pinks and blues. In the darkest part of the season this brings a soft sort of hope.

When Tess was young and the weather shifted, she was compelled to examine the past. She'd often sneak into her parents' "study," which they never seemed to enter. It was a perfect nook—a corner room with built-in bookshelves, a record player, a big green window coloured by the leaves outside, and a brown leather chair.

For her, this place was a temple. Not as sacred as her favourite climbing tree—her mother's American Beech tree—its beautiful roots surfacing out of the soil like clambering octopus arms, but a good substitute when she felt contemplative and couldn't go outside. She'd stare at the titles of her dad's political science textbooks: *Why Men Rebel, Man and Society*. She'd read books on

Ancient Egypt or the Second World War or, if she really wanted a thrill, she'd look at her mother's nursing textbooks, with their photos of genitalia and other terrifying realities.

She learned to respect history and secrets in that room, and to search silently for answers. Her parents were so lucky, objectively speaking, even if they were intensely unhappy. She wishes she had done more.

Her myopic view extended beyond her family. So many dark periods in history about which she was unaware. So much ignorance. How can she live with the knowledge of it? She hoped awareness would amount to atonement, but knows that it can't. Sometimes she needs to lie down.

Tess walks into a dark little hole otherwise known as the Café des échecs—dedicated to the game of chess. Funny that the word in French refers to the game, and once you remove the "s" it means "failure."

She senses she is playing a losing game with Mr. Hewitt.

A stench of wet mop and mould keeps assaulting her. The same black spongy mat would likely have been on this floor when people walked through here in the seventies. The smell of cigarettes isn't entirely absent, either, and it makes Tess feel as though she's gone back a few generations.

The only other patrons are old men. She won't run into anyone she knows here—not that she knows many people.

Tess listens to them for a little while, talking and joking as they have likely done for thirty years, waiting out the winter in this dank place until they can go outside and let the sun clean them out. She sips her coffee, which is quite good, and eats her chocolate cookie, which is quite stale. She can't help but notice that lots of people are drinking beer here. She knows no one would care, or notice, if she had one too.

She could finish the cookie and go back up to the cash. One beer wouldn't hurt.

Instead, she breathes. She takes out the letter that had fallen out of the book in Mr. Hewitt's hospital room. A letter he'd chosen to keep near him. A letter that she also stole.

A man in the café keeps belting out the words "Oh, Johnny" in a beautiful baritone, for no apparent reason. Perhaps it's a song, though he seems to sing at random intervals.

The song hardly registers as she approaches the contents of the letter. She senses she'll be transported into another time, another life, where she stands on a cliff, a threshold of love and suffering, breath bated, with the hope that the ending will be one of redemption.

She opens the letter carefully, spreading it out on top of a napkin so as not to dirty it. The handwriting is different from the rest of the journal. Brighter and neater, easier to read. It is in Spanish, but she can guess at the meaning most of the time, thanks to Mr. García.

She thinks of Jana's baby. She tries not to think about how old he would be now.

She pats the letter down, not wanting to touch it too much, not wanting to spread herself over it, but trying to coax out whatever truth might be lying in wait.

It was a day when you ordinarily would have come.

Sunday.

I wait for you at the plaza for three hours, feeling less exposed there than I would have in the park. Sitting on our bench I watch a little girl in a dirty dress and a polka-dot hat chasing pigeons. Waiting, smoking cigarettes. I feel a raindrop and count.

Uno, dos, tres.

I had loved you too late, perhaps, and before I knew it, you were gone. I know I made a mistake dating your friend, mistaking my fascination with his personality for love or desire. Being chosen by him made me feel strong. I know you two were friends. But there were layers of self-deception and misunderstanding. I was young, I didn't realize that he was also figuring out who he should be.

I want to tell you about the differences I feel lately, in my body, a process as simple and inexplicable as earth absorbing rainwater.

Now there are too many raindrops to count and the rain rebounds off an unforgiving pavement, shimmering, and I wonder if I should go. People are leaving the plaza, and I've been left alone with the woody smell of cigarettes in the rain—smoke and water. I feel the world in my body, on my shoulders. Your poems in my bag, next to my leaflets, and my weapon. I had always known what I wanted in life. My mother said I'd been born on a Wednesday, that odd day, and people born on that day were certain of themselves. But she wasn't there when I was born, so what does she know? I wanted to find my other parents. I wanted to be sure no one would walk all over me. I learned that thanks to Martín, yet here I find myself, in the rain, down to my last cigarette, in the plaza, waiting for a person who will never arrive.

I know you won't show, mi amor, *almost as well as I know you can't help it. It was not to be helped.*

I remain on the bench as people rush past, umbrellas and jackets and worry, and the rain increases in volume and persistence. Puddles form at my feet and, despite the looks received or the unsolicited advice to get home, I feel rooted to the spot because, and only because, it had been our meeting place. You sat on the bench with me, and this fills me with inexplicable, misplaced tenderness.

I loved you in a way that verged on maternal, perhaps because I believed my love to be unconditional. I wanted you only to be happy, and I knew there was little I could do to protect you. I knew you would leave me.

Perhaps I could feel that you had, little by little, disappeared like the wind scattering the leaves. "Hojas secas de otoño giraban en tu alma." My teacher and mentor had warned me—said you'd only disappoint. He didn't say it with cruel intention, either. That was the worst part. You simply derailed all my plans.

Love had felt so selfish. There was so much to do, yet there was an ache to be with you. It took me time to realize it.

Chapter 14

Tess finds Mr. Hewitt outside with the other patients, huddled together at picnic tables like scruffy pigeons. She calls out to him, waving her red mitten even though he can't see it. He gestures for her to come over as though he's seated in a cozy pub.

"I hate the winter. Don't you?" he says, as she approaches.

"I'm trying to love it," Tess lies. "I find a certain peace in the darkness and the cold."

"Ah, but it's never dark in the city now, is it? Besides, so many birds leave."

"That's true." And, as if on cue, a murder of black crows surfaces in the air nearby.

They listen to them for a moment, their calls urgent and foreboding.

"It's difficult to sleep sometimes. But you seem well, Mr. Hewitt."

Tess's breath forms white ribbons in the air, which mingle with Mr. Hewitt's exhalations of cigarette smoke. Two paths converging. If Tess can't sleep, it's not for the artificial light of the city, but for Mr. Hewitt and the mess she's gotten herself into, reading about his life.

The other patients shuffle to the hospital door, but Hewitt is still smoking.

"Whether I'm well or not is of no consequence. The truth is, I'm not sick, because I'm already dead. I've figured it all out. I just can't understand why people insist that I'm still here." He laughs. "Everyone here is crazy, Tess!"

Tess takes the seat next to him and watches the birds: sparrows, nuthatches, and chickadees. They form a semicircle around the picnic table which is covered in dirty snow and cigarette butts, as though listening to a sermon.

"Noah wants to place you in a group home," Tess says, gently. "He says it's really nice. Do you want me to ask him about it?"

He shakes his head. Tess waits for him to say something. He doesn't.

"Mr. Hewitt, could we talk some more about what happened to you?"

"You want to picture me when I was young and handsome."

"You're still handsome." She smiles. "No, I want to know more about that woman in the photo. Do you know where she is?"

He takes a sip of coffee and to Tess's surprise, he smiles. A smile from long ago, dredged out of his memory.

"She was wonderful, just wonderful."

The words blow through Tess like opening windows.

"I never did get to say goodbye. Though I don't imagine she would have wanted to see me, anyway," he says, scratching his head.

"Why not?" Even though she knows the answer, she just wants to hear him say it.

"She didn't like me. Well, she did, and then she didn't."

"Mr. Hewitt, why do you speak of her in the past tense?" Tess feels cruel asking this question.

Mr. Hewitt shakes his head.

"She's gone."

He looks at the sky.

"If I said her spirit talks to me, would you believe me?" he asks.

Instinctively Tess stands up, moves her feet to get some feeling back in her toes. The air strangles. She wipes crumbs off her pants. Grey everywhere—swirling in the clouds, in her eyes.

She sits down and Mr. Hewitt speaks again.

"In the end, all those things that I had in my apartment, my boxes ... well. It's because I cared."

Does he know she looked through his things? Perhaps it doesn't matter. She knows now their journeys are not linear.

"*Te recuerdo como eras en el último otoño,*" he says.

"Who do you remember, Mr. Hewitt?"

Who was the intended reader, who were the narrators?

What happened to them?

Were they real people, or was this all an invented story? A fantasy, someone's imagination, or the reflection of a symptom of whatever underlies Mr. Hewitt's mind and makes him believe that people want to poison him? She'd looked them up on the Internet, but had only found one person: *Esteban Repetto,* owner of a café. He fit the description in the journal, but so could so many.

She contacted him just in case he could tell her about this past, about these stories.

"Mr. Hewitt, in any case, you're not dead. You are here. I'm here. The doctors say you're—"

"What do they know? They think they're God. They think their shit doesn't stink."

"Mr. Hewitt. I don't think that's fair. You have great doctors. Besides, how do you explain me, if you're dead? How do you explain any of this?"

"I knew you'd say that. Being dead is like being in a dream—you know, the ones you can control. Or at least, the ones where you know what's coming next. Wise men, or women, speak because they have something to say; fools because they have to say something. Plato said that. I knew you'd say what you said."

"But that's because we've had this conversation before," she says. "Or because you know what I'm saying makes sense, even though I think you just called me a fool."

"Do you not think what I say makes sense?" he asks.

"Some of it does, yes."

"So why couldn't it be true?"

"Well, because only some of it makes sense—not all. We're going around in circles. Mr. Hewitt, I assure you you're not dead. I'm here, I'm alive, and I can see you."

"But that's just your perception of things. I've never had so many people in my life tell me that I'm wrong, when, for the first time in my life, I see things the way they really are. I see you."

She turns his words around in her head, trying to make sense of them, like a record that has finished playing, but continues its thudding, silent spin.

Chapter 15

Tess and Mr. Hewitt walk down St. Laurent, persecuted by the grey skies and a tightening cold that grabs them by the neck. Today he's wearing sneakers and a jacket that looks too thin for the weather. She asked him to put on an extra sweater, but he shrugged it off. The streets are mostly empty, and Tess guides him around construction pylons, electricity poles, and parking signs—his hand on her arm. They walk past a young man sitting on the street with his skinny German Shepherd. His hoodie covers most of the guy's face but his acne and matchstick legs give him away. A teenager. The days are colder and darker and Tess makes a note to buy him a sandwich on her way out.

Mr. Hewitt usually has the effect of calming her nerves. His ideas, words, and presence bring her out of her own life, but today she feels anxious. She has the feeling she's forgotten something. Perhaps her dream last night stayed with her, lingering on her skin, like a film she couldn't wash away. She'd dreamed of her mother at the beach, folding their towels, her auburn hair curling around her face from the salt air, her mouth a line. In the dream she saw her mother's usual expression, searching off in the distance for ... what?

In the dream, Tess enjoyed the sensations of the beach: the sand on her calves, pebbles between her toes, a trail of salt on her lips. In life, she was terrified of the ocean. In her dreams, she walked into the water like walking through a cloud. Easy, buoyant. No fear. Love. Then she saw a circle approaching in the water. White light, a halo, a body.

A face. A woman.

It occurs to her that dreams might be our memories coming back to haunt us. Or someone else's memories.

She invites Mr. Hewitt to her new spot, the Café des échecs, since this was the place where she'd read Bárbara's note. It was here that she witnessed the indisputable proof that Mr. Hewitt had been loved.

They enter and she describes the café. She tells him about the mismatched aluminum tables and chairs, and about the amateur paintings on the walls and the retro advertisements for Coca-Cola and cigarettes. It pains her that he can't see any of it. She wonders how it feels—to be trapped in sound.

She stands in line to buy his tea, and watches him as he sits and waits for her. His hands are on the table, face down, and he sits very straight.

She brings him his tea with a splash of cream. She's going to take a risk today.

Her heart beats fast. As she sits, she asks him, "Did you know that a secret can kill you, if you don't give it away?" Words from the journal. Will they have an effect? She watches his face for any sign of recognition. His unseeing eyes look beyond her shoulder. He raises his heavy eyebrows.

"What secrets are you keeping, my dear?" he says.

He doesn't understand the hint.

She searches in her mind for a secret she can share. She stirs her coffee, even though there's nothing in it. It is black, bitter water.

"This tea's horrible," he says, taking slurpy sips. "So, what's your secret?"

"Well, I was hoping you might want to share with me, but I can go first. A few years ago I saw myself, or a version of myself, at my mother's funeral," Tess says.

"Ah yes, the double."

"Pardon?"

He smiles, and it lights his face.

"Borges described them as beings that emerge in dreams and fantasy. He talked about the origin of ideas, and since the whole universe is one living thing, then there is kinship in all things. Even our imaginations. Even in the mystery that we are to ourselves."

"I'm not sure I understand."

"It's possible that you're searching for yourself. The double is inspired by mirrors. Have you looked in a mirror lately?"

Someone at the next table looks over at them. She supposes this could sound like an insult. She smiles and touches her hair.

"Uh, yes I have. But it doesn't help me explain this woman. She wasn't in any reflection. She looked like me, in the sense that she is my height, my weight, has my hair colour and eye colour, a certain expression around the mouth. But she was a different person."

"Did anyone else see her? Could they confirm she looked like you? Do you know what you look like? The Oracle at Delphi said 'know thyself,' but then, of course, Oscar Wilde said 'only the shallow know themselves.'"

He takes another sip of tea.

"Mr. Hewitt, you are incredible. How do you remember all this? Do you remember everything you ever read?"

"Having a good memory means you're always begrudging how stupid you once were."

She laughs, and seizes her opportunity.

"I wonder if you also remember events from your childhood? What about your friends, when you were a young man?"

He pauses for a moment, and his eyebrows furrow, forming a kind of triangular shape above his eyes.

"How could I remember it all? My remembered selves are as strange to me as strangers. We believe our image to be stable, but we're constantly in flux. Only by communicating to myself, perhaps, writing everything down, would I come close to some indication of who I have been."

She's glad he can't see her guilty face. She can't believe how lucid he seems today.

He raises a thick finger.

"The final option, the most likely one, is that this is an ominous sign. In some places, seeing yourself meant that your *Doppelgänger* was on his or her way to bring you to your death."

She wonders if it is a coincidence that the mystery woman showed up at her mother's funeral. Was she there to call Tess to her death? Did a part of her die when her mother died?

"But don't worry. In truth, the double is just your conscience. The person that you shall never be. Now, are we going to play chess or not?"

Later, when Tess is alone, she folds laundry with a bottle of wine at her side, listening to Jana's road-trip-music mixtape, her mind wandering, thinking about Mr. Hewitt in the hospital. What is he doing now?

She thinks again of their conversation about the double. The person she is not and will never be. Could she be someone who is solid, hard, and capable? Is this person the version of Tess that her mother wanted her to be? The one that wasn't too sensitive or too dreamy? Is she the version of Tess that could move through the world without feeling people's pain as her own?

More urgently, did she invent this woman who looks like her? How secure are her own memories? What does it mean that she can't recall her mother's voice?

After they finished their chess game, they sat in silence. She wondered if he mentioned writing because he was aware she'd stolen his journal. She nudged him gently. He responded that language was meant to bridge the barrier between our perception of the world and someone else's. He said we rely on words to exchange abstractions, but silence is better.

"Sometimes your deepest emotions, if shared with the wrong people, can feel cheap. Don't you find? People turn to religion, politics, sex, drugs, work, astrology, dream interpretation— anything to convince us that our interactions have greater meaning than basic survival," he had said. "And look. Consider this. I need you to tell me where you're moving on the chess board, and I trust you. That's it, that's all."

The doorbell rings. He stands on the step, rumpled and grey. Her father.

"Dad, what on earth? What are you doing here?"

"I know, Tessie. I'm sorry to do this to you, I would have given you a heads-up, but I had to come in person and I was afraid you'd be worried if I told you I was on my way. Okay if I come in?"

He's winded and crinkled-looking. Tess takes his duffel bag and leads him in. He looks smaller than he used to, more bent, though it's only been a few months since she last saw him.

Jana is in the kitchen, and Tess introduces them. Her dad knows Jana's parents. Tess feels hot. Her face is red. She tells her dad to wait in the living room while she makes him a cup of coffee.

Then she apologizes to Jana.

"I had no idea he was coming."

"Tess, don't worry. So nice to see someone from home. I was on my way out, anyway." Jana enfolds her in a hug for which Tess feels unworthy. Then Jana grabs her purse and jacket on some pretense of an errand and leaves the apartment. Tess is left with her father in the living room.

"Tessie, what a great apartment you have here. And to live with a nice girl like Jana. She's so glamorous! That's wonderful."

"Yeah, it's nice. I miss you, though." It's true. She wouldn't have been able to imagine her father in this apartment an hour earlier, but he looks settled in the bean bag. The fact that he is wearing his favourite wool sweater that he's worn her entire life provokes a sort of spell; a reminder of a feeling from before, as though a younger, more innocent and optimistic version of Tess is floating protectively over her head.

"You look good, Dad." Though he looks smaller, he still seems slim and healthy enough. He probably still spends every afternoon at the wharf.

"Thanks, Tessie. I'm hanging in there. Listen, I'll cut to the chase."

He looks into his coffee.

Tess leans forward.

He scratches his neck.

"Okay, I was contacted by a woman lately."

Tess nods.

"Well, let me start at the beginning. Your mother ..." Tears swell in his eyes. She's not used to this. Stiff upper lip and all that.

"Yes?" Her heart is pounding.

"Well, she never told you this, but some guy got your mother pregnant when she was just seventeen, so young." He shakes his head.

She waits.

"Her parents sent her to Montreal to have the baby."

He looks at her.

"That's what people did in those days." His eyes plead with her not to judge. "Your poor mother was obliged to give the baby away."

He loved her mother so much.

"And the baby, well, she grew up here."

"The double ..." Tess says.

"What? She was adopted by a nice family. She had a good life. Her name is Marie, though your mother had called her Mary. Marie looked for your mother, but by the time she found her, she was already too late. Your mother had just passed away."

Marie.

Her father places his thumb and pointer finger on his eyes.

Tess sits next to the bean bag and places her head on her father's arm.

"I'm sorry you've been dealing with this alone. Why did Mum never tell me?"

"She thought it would be too upsetting for you." He takes a sip of coffee and chokes a little. Tess can't seem to bring her thoughts together. Her mind is blank, as though someone shook an Etch A Sketch and the lines all disappeared. "It was difficult for her to talk about. In fact, I promised her I would never tell you about Mary. Marie."

"Why are you telling me then?"

"Well, she came looking for us. Marie wants to meet you."

Tess feels a surge of panic.

"She's adamant, in fact," he adds.

Tess had already said goodbye to her mother. She doesn't think she can handle this emotional upheaval too.

"I'm not sure I can meet her right away. I have a lot going on," she says.

"I understand, Tessie, I just wanted to be the one to tell you. I didn't want her to track you down without any warning. I'll let Marie know that you need some time."

They decide to go for a walk, and her dad marvels at all the restaurants, stores and excitement just beyond her front door. Tess wonders what else her mother kept from her. It's often a shock for children to realize that their parents had lives before they were born, though Tess has always known there was something about her mother's life that she'd never be able to fix.

Tess offers to buy her father a chocolate milkshake and they chat in the diner, but her mind is tugging thoughts from the sky down to the pit of her stomach. All the *if onlys* that her mother must have also turned around in her own head like devotion. Like a wound she would have kept reopening. Perhaps her mother hadn't wanted to replace Marie by loving Tess. Perhaps Tess could have grown up with a sister and a happy mother. Perhaps Marie could have been the fourth point of their family compass.

Chapter 16

Tess is waiting for Noah in the community room. He's in a staff meeting, discussing Mr. Hewitt's future, and he's promised to fill her in afterwards. She fingers the brochure of Mr. Hewitt's group home. Photos of an Indigenous man with a suit and brief-case (as though a corporate job were the measure of success), an older couple with startlingly white teeth, and a mixed-race family smile at her as they stand at the entrances of their new, subsidized homes.

She's worried for Mr. Hewitt, but the place looks lovely. It is a family-type residence, the brochure explains, structured around a non-professional caregiving model, with supervision in connection with hospital-based teams.

Noah had said they'd chosen this home because it wasn't far from the hospital, and Mr. Hewitt would stay in a familiar neighbourhood. He would be monitored and supported, even given small jobs. Residents would be encouraged to take turns buying groceries, cooking, and cleaning.

"He'll need a library card with access to books. Preferably braille books and audio books, but he also likes it when some-one reads to him," she'd told him.

Two nurses walk through the community room then, speak-ing in French about some patients who were found making out in their rooms. They're laughing.

Tess feels a sadness on her chest as the doctors and Noah emerge from a back room. Dr. Weintraub is the head psychiatrist on Mr. Hewitt's file. As Dr. Weintraub talks to Noah, she smoothes an eyebrow with a long, pink fingernail.

Tess struggles to listen. They're talking about medication. She hears the words "antipsychotics and anxiolytics." She hears them bounce words like Clozaril, Zyprexa, Seroquel back and forth for a few moments. Dr. Weintraub's holiday tan and sleeveless shirt look odd in the community room, with her biceps bulging like dinner rolls.

"Let's go to rounds. I need a coffee," Dr. Weintraub says, stretching her long, lean legs. She looks so tired.

Then Noah walks over to Tess, smiling. He's holding a file in his hand. It's Mr. Hewitt's file.

"It went well. All is going according to plan," he says. "If we can get Martin to cooperate, then we don't need to go to court."

Tess zooms in on a stain on Noah's collar. She notices a mole on his chin. She sees his eyes are slightly different colours.

She has trouble finding her voice.

"What did you say?"

"I said we won't need to go to court, if he cooperates."

"If who cooperates?"

"Martin. Mr. Hewitt."

Noah looks at his watch.

"I need to go to rounds, but I wondered if you wanted to break the news to him."

Tess looks slowly at the file and sees it. As though a bullseye surrounds it. The small white label with the printed name.

A large "M."

M for misleading, mocking, murderer.

M for Martín.

She's angry. All this time, she thought she was talking to Andrés, and he turned out to be Martín. Why the fuck does she try to help people? Why is she worrying about this man, about whom she knows nothing, whose father sounds like he was in bed with dictators and who was a terrible person? Why isn't she worried about her own father, or this new sister who has just come into her life? Why can't she just live her life and be happy with her friends? Why didn't she tell Cam how she felt? Why can't she be a normal, grown-up person?

Why has she wasted so much time on fucking Martín Hewitt, when he couldn't even be honest with her?

Jana is staying at Hari's place. Tess is ignoring messages from Cam, Olivier, and Tony. She texted Astrid to let her know she's fine, but she just needs a little time.

She has ten missed calls.

She opens a beer, then another, and then switches to Scotch. She opens her desk drawer, removing the woman's photo. The woman's eyes are confident, giving the impression she's ready to challenge a world she's certain will let her down. Tess knows her name—Bárbara. And she knows Mr. Hewitt, whoever he was, was in love with this Bárbara Bianchi. That much is clear as daylight. But he also caused her death.

She opens her computer and types "Disappeared, Operation Condor." The first website, the *Wall of Memory,* confronts her— hundreds of black and white photos. There is an option to click on the photos and read each obituary, some with explanations of the disappearance or information about the death itself.

Dozens of faces. Young men and women in the prime of life. Some older people who likely thought they'd already lived through the worst of it all. She thinks of the concentric circles of agony and grief radiating outwards from these hearts.

The weight of it all forces her down onto her bed. A heaviness sits on her chest, a pain emanating from knowledge, from the certainty of suffering. This pain is not even hers, yet she lives inside it like a squatter in a rundown house. She can't fathom the suffering committed in the name of progress and civilization, or this narrow perspective on the myriad ways people can thrive. Money and power. Here, there, and everywhere. All the blood spilled, and for what? She feels like the beneficiary of it all, with her perfect life. It all comes down to her, at the end of the line, and what has she done with it?

Cam imagines a world of love. Jana creates despite the hole in her heart. Olivier has the courage to care for others. Tony teaches the truth.

The truth. She laughs and takes another gulp.

How could anyone ever know all the truth?

She never imagined that life could be different. She always accepted the status quo, where good and evil, light and dark, were presented as distinct. She never imagined they were actually blurred together in the half-light.

When she was younger she believed people were good. She believed even if they did bad things, she would be able to bring their inherent goodness to the surface.

How insecure, yet incredibly self-centered, can one person be?

She needs to know what happened to Andrés, though she wonders if she's wasting her time, causing herself pain for no reason. She wonders if she's losing her mind. But she gets off her bed and returns to the computer.

She scrolls. She drinks.

Of course she sees her, or thinks she does. The face is grainy and in the photo she's not smiling—but it is Bárbara. That same straight hair parted right in the middle, the same fine cheekbones and determined expression. Tess's cursor hangs over the photo. She clicks it.

Fecha de desaparición - 06/1978: Bianchi Santorini, Bárbara (Encinta).

A quick online translation confirms her suspicion. She can't explain how she knew it even before she saw the parenthesized words. Tess jumps up, unable to thaw the ice chilling her skin. Bárbara had been pregnant when she disappeared.

She remembers the first thing he'd said when she saw him in the hospital: sanity is absurd. Maybe he's right. Maybe none of this story makes sense. Maybe none of her story makes sense.

She stays in and pours herself coffee in the kitchen. Steam rises and dissipates like a person's strength. She adds Scotch. He'd said it was about trust. He trusted her to tell him where she put her chess pieces. And she'd trusted him to be the person she thought he was.

It feels as though other parts of her life have fallen away, and she is faced only with the memories and dreams of this man whose history she could neither fathom nor hope to decipher. Archives. Names and photos. Photo with no name. Name with no photo. Who are these people?

Constellations.

We think someday we'll touch that beautiful horizon, the blurry light between sea and sky. She tells Jana that memories are haunting her, and the past is a predator. She says we move forward and back, bending time in our minds, using memory like a balm. But it is a bomb. People who are gone from the world visit us in words and dreams. They trick our minds to convince us they're still here. Only the lines on our faces, the pains in our bodies, and their aching absences render the stark reality. Change is time's friend and it is, after all, the only constant in life.

A text from Cam.

It is not enough to save someone else. It should save you too, but it doesn't always.

She looks through the papers she printed at the library about trauma and memory. She borrowed books about dictatorships in the 1970s. She knocks them all off the desk and falls over. She cuts her thumb. What does she know? How can these papers capture the blood and tears? Where are the band-aids? How will she ever understand?

As she walks in the cold, it hits her: she never felt a true connection here, never felt the history. She just felt like a lonely person walking along dirty streets. She passes grey people, their resentment piercing through her. The tacky clothes in the window of a dusty store assault her eyes; the crowds and noise ravage her ears. Everyone just trying to make the most of their lives, each one with their unique sad story that she will not change.

All these people who look for another, better life are suddenly cast in a new light. They seem like victims of a conspiracy—all together—one that convinces people to keep moving and growing; to rip tender, tentative roots out of the earth. A quiet genocide, the pervasiveness and persistence of supremacy and shame, a thousand deaths of sacred words lost to the wind. The only way out is conformity. Right and wrong become reversed or simply blurred in the wind and the tears.

Olivier may be right.

She's meeting him in front of Our Lady of the Harbour. Notre-Dame-de-Bon-Secours Chapel. She approaches the St. Lawrence; the river is a blade. No sun, no honey. The poetry, even in its contradictions, seems a pretense. No star of the sea. No meaning.

She walks slowly up to Olivier. Suddenly his tongue is arrogantly searching her mouth.

She is angry and pushes him away.

She sits on the bench surrounded by potted flowers and Olivier stands nearby. He's talking but she can't hear him. She's focused on a pile of trash spilling out of the garbage can nearby: A Tim Horton's coffee cup, a carton of Chinese food with some leftovers inside, a plastic knife, a baby diaper. Next to her feet, a pile of dog shit and cigarette butts.

She rocks back and forth. She is crying. The clock tower ticks away, reminding her that change is the only constant, though she knows time is one of those human fantasies that is both real and not. What does it mean to be a witness?

"You're right, Olivier, we are products now. We are a monotonous set of soulless shadows. Disconnected and interchangeable. We don't want to be implicated. They ask us every day to change, through our dreams, to be better, and we can't."

Olivier is calling someone on the phone.

Mr. Hewitt never said he'd written the journal. He never told her who he was. She was so focused on her own life, and how it intersected with his, she never even took the time to ask him his first name.

How do people go on eating, drinking, sleeping, when it doesn't matter what they do, factors beyond their control can determine their destiny? She wants to access her mind. Perhaps that is all she can control. She stays in her room. She thinks if she analyzes memories, dreams, desires, she may come to understand the vastness of the self. Of her self.

Yet she knows it's a privilege to contemplate anything at all.

She wakes. She hears Jana speaking to someone from the hallway. A glass of water and a bowl of soup sit on her bedside table. Tess's mouth is parched. She's been talking out loud.

The stars. Even the ones we see may no longer exist. We're seeing their past. Tess thinks it's the same for people. Maybe they're no longer here, but we see them anyway.

She dreams.

More vivid than ever. She's surrounded by shades of blue and green, broken through with refracted columns of light from above. She's not wet, but she's under water. She floats. Her hair is weightless. It sways gently on her head like seaweed. She can move her limbs freely and with ease, and she can breathe. The water moves in and out of her mouth like heavy air, she tastes the salt.

Once it's established—the fact that she can breathe—she realizes she can't see well. Blurry shadows brush through her line of vision, but she can't make them out.

Then a baby. Her own baby. Her smiling face. Her needs, so huge. Her love, so clear. So clear. Her eyes, bright and real. Her body. Sun catching on her hair. Sun reflecting in her eyes. Baby teeth. Hands and feet. Floating. Floating. Lifting arms up to her, needing her, loving Tess, loving her. So much love. So much need. Life is changed forever because the baby needs Tess. Because she needs her.

Tess wakes, like climbing towards the sun. Groggy. She is confused, but at least she's in her own bed. She checks her phone.

A few missed calls from her dad.

Messages from Astrid.

An email from Cam.

A voicemail from Olivier.

A link to an article from Tony, along with a cow emoji inviting her on a date.

Ten missed calls from Noah, Mr. Hewitt's social worker. She calls him back.

Mr. Hewitt is all settled in now. He asked Noah to find Tess.

Noah begs Tess to see him. He says it's part of his "recovery." He says Tess knows Mr. Hewitt more than anyone else.

She doesn't know him at all.

But she agrees that she needs to speak to him. She grabs her metro pass, takes a pill for her headache, pulls on her boots, and heads out.

The townhouse of the group home is virtually indistinguishable from the line of red residential houses, although the garden is better tended and there is a small blue sign on the front window with a sun on it. The caregiver welcomes her in French and shows her around. The minimalist, Nordic vibe is comforting. White, clean lines and forest-green trim, pale wood. Softly institutional. The caregiver, Sébastien, tells her that they stick to their routine like glue.

Before they reach Mr. Hewitt's room, she hears him. He's yelling. She catches snatches of words.

"Someone must have taken it, then! It is the only thing that matters to me and someone has taken it."

Her pulse is a drum beat.

"Mr. Hewitt, Mr. Hewitt. Just a moment, and I can help you. Please stop yelling, so I can understand you." Someone has rushed to his room to calm him down.

"It is a book, goddamn it! I need it!"

The caregiver suggests to Tess that she should come back later. She ignores him.

Tess opens the door to his room while the caregiver hovers behind her. Mr. Hewitt is pacing, slowly, in an empty room. Her heart aches, but then she remembers that he is Martín. His tears are guilty ones, originating from a fear of being called out. She feels no pity.

"Hi, Mr. Hewitt. It's me," she says, her mouth dry.

"Tess?" He stops pacing and looks in her direction. He seems so relieved to hear her voice that she can't help but soften a little. But she's here on business.

"Do you want to go out for a bit?" she asks, more kindly than she intended.

"I'd love that, Tess. But I lost something and these people can't tell me where it is. It's the only thing that matters to me. It's the only thing I want to keep."

"Mr. Hewitt, I went through your apartment with you, and I remember you saying there was nothing that you wanted to keep. You said there were just shards of memory or something like that."

"Well, I don't have to tell you everything, do I?" Mr. Hewitt says.

"No, but I was helping you."

"Even someone as needy as I has a right to their own business." Tess's knees buckle a little.

"You're right. But I have to tell you something. Could we go for a walk? Make sure you dress warm enough."

It is a sunny, windy day. They make their way down the street in silence. Their boots crunch and squeak through the snow. Tess waits until they've walked a ways before speaking.

"Mr. Hewitt, you said something about sincerity being a condition for friendship. I considered you my friend, and that's why I have to tell you that I have your journal."

A beat.

"I have to sit down," he says, slowly.

Tess leads him to a park bench and he sits down, removing his arm from hers. She waits. She watches him, but his expression is vacant. She waits some more.

"Mr. Hewitt, I'm sorry I took your journal."

She doesn't hear any birds today.

"I'm also sorry to learn that you're Martín."

He swivels his head to look at her, and it seems as though he locks eyes with her.

Then he puts his head in his hands. He sighs. He sniffs.

"So you read everything?" he asks.

"Yes. And I'm sorry for that."

"You're always sorry, goddamn it!"

"You're right. I am. I am sorry. But I'm also concerned. I'd like to know what happened, if you'd be willing to tell me. What happened to Andrés? Was he killed too?"

"Why the hell do you need to know? What happened to you? You don't see me sticking my head into your business!"

Mr. Hewitt scratches his head under his tuque, and sits up with his gloved hands on his knees. He stares straight ahead towards the street, where buses and cars plow through the wet snow.

He sighs.

"Tess, you have to understand. Andrés incriminated himself. He incriminated her, too."

"How?"

A bus stops in front of them, and a woman with a huge stroller struggles to embark. Tess rushes to help her, and then sits back down.

"I don't actually know, but he went to Martín's house, my house, and said something to my mother that made her suspicious."

"He had good reason to be afraid of her, if what the journal said is true," Tess says, then realizes Mr. Hewitt might resent her insulting his mother.

"Yes, well. She was lonely. Doesn't excuse it. Turns out my father was having an affair with Andrés's mother."

Tess inhales sharply. It is so odd to hear these names coming from Mr. Hewitt's mouth. It makes them seem more real.

"So my father was angry about what he said, but I begged that Andrés be allowed to go free. My father decided to help him. He made a few phone calls. He decided to help Bárbara as well, but it was ..."

His voice caught.

"It was too late."

Tess feels a lump in her throat. She wants to believe him, but she knows they likely got rid of Bárbara because she was more "dangerous" or because she could give them more names.

"But I see her everywhere."

"You see her?" Tess asks.

He waves his hand. "You know, you know. I feel as though I see her. I sense her. The other day I sensed her standing at the entrance of the Metro. I immediately thought 'how confusing for her—she doesn't know the city. How will she get to where she's going?' Instead of wondering how on earth I might be seeing her. I'm so used to it. She looked at me as though I had made no promise and her face held no expectation. She lives in a place now where time is not measured, so maybe I have a chance yet," he said.

"A chance for what, Mr. Hewitt?"

"A chance to do better. The admiral, my father, was worried about me should the story ever get out, so he sent me away."

They sit in silence. An ambulance siren goes off in the distance. He is crying.

214

"I'm so sorry, Mr. Hewitt. I'm sorry I made you speak about this. We don't have to talk about it again if you don't want to."

She leads him home.

*

There's a message.

From Esteban—the friend with the loud laugh. He answered her message. She had told him she was doing research, and wanted to know what happened to people who had disappeared.

Hello, good to hear from you. I'm glad people in Canada are interested in our history. My friends were special people. I include below a link to an article written by Bárbara, when she was detained, before she died. You can read her words. It is very sad what happened to her. So many lives cut short.

I miss my friends.

Best,

Esteban Repetto.

She can't read the article just yet. She can see that Esteban is still connected, there's a little green light next to his name. She writes:

Thank you, Esteban, for answering me. I will read the article written by Bárbara. I just have a quick question, because I neglected to mention earlier that my interest in this period of history, and specifically in your friends, stems from a journal that I read. It belonged to Andrés. I came across it almost by accident. I wonder if you could tell me what happened to him?

...

Ah, my friend Andrés. He was a writer. It doesn't surprise me that he had a journal. He and Bárbara had a love that made us all envious.

But his story is mysterious. No one knows where he went. We think his mother sent him away. He may have had relatives in other countries.

...

Maybe Martín knows. We've become friends. We met when I delivered food to him. I am trying to gain his trust so he'll tell me what happened to Andrés.

It seems as though Esteban is typing for an eternity. Typing and erasing what he writes.

...

Pardon? Martín?

...

Yes, Martín Hewitt. He lives here now.

...

...

...

That's impossible. Martín is dead.

...

...

He cannot be in Canada. He died thirty years ago.

Chapter 17

Dearest Tess,

Now I write to you. It is possible I always have.

I'm leaving tomorrow. I won't see you before I go, so I need to clear the air, as they say.

First permit me the indulgence of some ramblings. Today, I was able to walk through the city, to revel in the euphoria of spring. It is something people can't understand, can they, unless they live through winter in this place? 'Mon pays, ce n'est pas un pays, c'est l'hiver.' Is this my country? Perhaps it has become so. Our hearts have infinite space for new people as for new landscapes, I think. Would you agree?

Today, though, this country was rebirth. Everything I encountered signaled endurance and life, luminescence and light. A beautiful operatic woman's voice serenaded me from an open window, lifting up and up as though climbing a sunbeam. I passed a playground where a group of children, teenagers, and parents openly shared laughter and joy. And of course, my birds are returning from the south, just as I embark on the opposite journey. I wished you'd been with me today.

Perhaps it was my frame of mind, since you've helped me. We shared a story for a while, didn't we? But whose story is it, and what right does either of us have to it?

We must be wary of personal stories; we are unreliable narrators of our own experiences. But did you know that "narration" derives from the Latin "gnarus," meaning "to recognize or know?"

My dear Tess, you recognized in me someone worth knowing. Why did you take the time, when it takes so much time, to weave a web of connection with a lonely old man? Perhaps we are connected by the ties of love and grief, which are essentially the same. Like stone, we can be shifted, striated, or eroded in time—either way, we are never the same. Perhaps we understand one another.

I'm sure someone has told you you're too soft. The world should be softer.

It would be nice to think that right and wrong are nuanced. Perhaps we think this because there is no objective reality; we are merely tied to our subjective perceptions. Yet we all know that right and wrong are real. Though I am not a particularly religious person, despite my mother's teachings, I still believe that there is goodness in the world, and I know it when I sense it. Like my grandmother did. It lives in the trees, in the birds, and in our love for one another. We make excuses for the past in order to continue on with our lives.

You've been asking me about my past, which is as imagined as my future. One thing we learn with time is that it is dangerous to stay in either place, but it is particularly dangerous to linger on our memories. Memory can be distorted. Memory can haunt.

Moving forward is the only truth.

Camus said you will never live if you are looking for the meaning of life. You, Tess, seek meaning in everything—this is lovely. You have tried to understand what happened to me, and in the process, to help me. I know that was your intention. Though some might be chagrined at the interference, I am touched.

I may not have been honest last time when we spoke.

I have learned that so much in life relates to perception, and the kaleidoscope of the self. Turn this way, you'll appear in such a way; angle yourself forty-five degrees to the right, you'll be different. It is about perception. The little girl won't be perceived the same way by her classmates as by her parents, by the librarian, or by the younger boy down the street. All the sides of yourself will never come together, because they belong to the other. And the others' perceptions more often relate to themselves than they do to you. Yet there is a truth to you, which cannot be denied.

I will get to the point. I want to explain why I wrote everything down. I wanted my version to be recorded.

You, in your questioning, have given me the answer to a second chance. Like a caged bird, I must now flee. Is home where you return, or where you begin? Or the in-between? I depart relieved and frightened, and bursting with a gratitude that I have difficulty expressing in a manner worthy of my feeling. Esteban will meet me at the airport.

Tess, you told me about Clara. I need to tell you now that your mother may have been more like you than you realize. She may have been unable to confront the cruelty of the world, and wanted to shield you from it. She may have come to the conclusion, like Don Quixote, that if you make yourself into honey, the flies will devour you. She may have given up, and lost her light.

Please don't give up. Do you know that I will find Clara? Though I have no expectations. She may not want anything to do with me, which I would understand, because I suspect we can choose a family with greater ease than we can accept our own blood.

Perhaps you are my family.

We want to believe we are separate, but that is an illusion. Love will stay.

I want you to know some of the truths. What do I mean? Bárbara admired a Cuban singer, Silvio Rodríguez, who asked,

"Hasta dónde debemos practicar las verdades?" *There, he asked what to do when two of our intrinsic values enter into contradiction with one another.*

I will sign off here. Thank you for all you've done for me. Before I go, I want to leave you with the end of my story, which is not entirely my story, for what it's worth.

Imagine your father is furious about the fact that you lost your eyesight. Imagine he wants to kill you because of the actions and associations of your friends. You had merely followed your friend to see what he was up to. You know where the girlfriend lives, you have it written down, but you're worried that your father will have them both killed. It is well known that your father, the admiral, has no pity.

What do you do?

You can't see, but you try to grab the paper with the address from his huge hand, to burn it with the lighter, which is always next to the ashtray.

You fumble around, but don't succeed. You try the next line of defence. You get on your knees and beg.

The father screams, "Look what they've done to you! Be a man!"

He thinks you're brainwashed, but you aren't. You are on his side, for the most part, yet you still love your friends. You are practicing your truths.

You forced your friend to give you the information. You tricked him.

You were convinced what they were doing was wrong.

You decide to fight force with force. You'll show him you're a man. You grab the real revolver, in the closet, and you hold it, under your chin. You tell your father that you will kill yourself before allowing him to hurt your friends.

Your father approaches you. You hope he's scared. You hope he's terrified. You mean it. You'll do it. You can't see, but you sense him. He's large and smells like whisky, cologne, and sweat. At the last moment, you try to free your arm from his, but as you do, your finger inadvertently pulls the trigger.

Chapter 18

"So Martín killed himself?"

"By accident, yes."

"But he had been the one to denounce Bárbara? I mean, he led them to her house?"

"Yes, but afterwards he tried to save her, it seems. And Andrés, too."

"So Andrés got away, but she was detained anyway?" Jana asks. She sits on Tess's bed, a cup of tea and box of Kleenex in her hand.

"It seems Martín's father was sick with grief and remorse, and he told Mr. Hewitt—Andrés—to pretend to be Martín. He gave Mr. Hewitt Martín's passport, clothes, and money. They wanted to send him away where he could begin a new life. His mother and grandmother would go elsewhere, so no one would figure out what happened. Andrés was also sick with grief. He blamed himself."

Tess's throat tightens up.

"And he pretended to be Martín, until he started to believe he really was him."

"Was he pretending to be blind, too?" Jana asks.

"I guess so. Maybe he was in so much pain, he felt he couldn't see. Or no one could see him."

"Only you. You saw him, and he could see you."

Tess smiles at Jana and takes her hand.

Chapter 19

They make their way down the street, arm in arm. His feels strong and warm. Their reflections in a shop window return their gaze, admiring their good looks and easy laughter.

Where she'd felt an immediate, soulful friendship with Cam and an intellectual challenge in her discussions with Olivier, she thinks it might take longer to know Tony. Not that he's not attractive—in fact, she can't ignore the urge to place her hands on his broad chest. Since she met him, she's been fighting the allure of his sensuality, which dozes in his eyes, his mouth, his carriage, his voice. But that first night, when she unbuttoned her blouse to his eager, cautious hands, she'd felt awkward, as though they weren't really responding to desire, but playing a part.

She'd also experienced a moment of concern, always at the back of her mind with a man whose heart and mind is not fully unveiled to her. But she's happy they've passed that hurdle, for now. They talk about books they've read, movies they've seen. Safe, rather boring subjects.

Inside the club, they sit on plush red seats. He orders cocktails. He didn't ask her if she liked jazz. She's not a fan. She sits through the intimate performance, clapping after every solo, nodding, feeling a fuzzy contentment, thinking about the people around her. All these containers for pain and sorrow, joy and love.

She thinks about Mr. Hewitt, and wishes he were there with her.

When the show is over, they walk the cold blue sidewalk talking about music. After the stuffiness of the jazz club, the air is invigorating and they agree they could walk all night. Through a steamy window, Brazilian rhythms and percussion command their attention, and they enter a small, steamy club.

Tony smiles when she buys him a drink. He places his arm around her and tells her in her ear (he almost has to yell over the music), that he hopes she understands he's not looking for anything serious right now. He's just trying to have fun after a difficult separation. The words, coming as they do with a warm, sensual rush in her ear, confuse her.

She'd been so pleased with herself for moving on. She'd found a job in social work along the lines of community organizing, she'd sent Cam and Rita a gift for their baby, and she'd signed up for swim lessons.

Mr. Hewitt taught her about his life through these memories whose veracity she can never verify. She had tried to understand the details of the pain and guilt, but in the end the enduring emotion was his love and forgiveness. In the end, and against all odds, she felt closer to Mr. Hewitt than anyone else.

He'd even sent her a photo of Clara. She has the same determined look as her mother.

Tony pulls her onto the dance floor. Others bounce and shake all around them, the contagion of free movement and unchoreographed joy. Tess slowly lets herself move with him. Suddenly the startling wetness of Tony's mouth. She closes her eyes and sees points of light behind pink eyelids. He puts his hands on her hips, moving them in figure eights, and she—separate from her body—can do nothing but follow.

Martín hadn't been innocent in the story, but he also hadn't betrayed his friends. Not really. Mr. Hewitt, Andrés, had collected and contained his memories, his grief and guilt, and love, until it almost destroyed him. But it hadn't.

Back in the bar, Tess asks for a glass of water. Tony leaves, but she decides to stay. She is sad, but at least it's her own sadness. She texts Marie: can't wait to see you at brunch tomorrow, and Marie answers immediately with a smiley face and heart.

Tess still feels like dancing. She dances alone as the rhythm moves her. An ancestral pulse, like a single beat in a chorus of human hearts.

Fin

Acknowledgements

Thank you to Robin Philpot and Baraka Books for all your work in making this dream a reality. Many thanks to Licia Cantor, Elise Moser and Blossom Thom for insightful edits. A most special thank you to my dear friend, Lucia Granados, for designing the perfect cover.

I have been fortunate for the support of so many who have a long-standing place in my heart, even if we have been separated by distance or time. I wish I could include everyone here.

Thank you to the Humber Program in creative writing and David Adams Richards, who patiently guided me in writing very early drafts.

Thank you to all my professors and friends at Chatham University, in particular Sarah Shotland and Marc Nieson, for helping me to consider the structure of this novel and for compelling me to dig deeper. To Paul Bilger, many of our exchanges helped to shape the text. I also want to thank Sherrie Flick, Lori Jakiela, Sheila Squillante, and Sheryl St. Germain for being teachers and so much more. Also, Brittany Hailer, Leila Zonouzi, Alex Friedman, Kat Knuth, Kelsey Leach, Rachel Kaufman, Kelly Kepner, Stephanie Vega, Sharla Yates, Beth Royce and so many others are incredible friends and mentors and I'm so lucky to have met you all.

I am grateful to my Ottawa writing group, as well as colleagues in IILA and at Books on Beechwood, who encouraged me every step of the way.

Thank you to Alex Wenham—my first reader in Paris—and to friends who read early, painful drafts and convinced me to keep going. Claudio y Gina, gracias por los consejos. Special thanks to Sophie for always inspiring me.

A mi familia Ecuatoriana, y a los que viven en NH, incluyendo a Naíma y Ofelia, me siguen inspirando con su amor sin límite. A los amigos de Costa Rica, sobre todo Gabriela Rodríguez y Gustavo Briceño, gracias por enseñarme tanto. Thank you to my extended family in NS and NB for all the wonderful summers. Extra love to JJ, and thank you to the Moquette family for being my home away from home.

Some people, including Tianna Dagher, Lucia Granados, Jasmine Abella, Alex Mahony and Dominique Potvin need special mention owing to our twenty-five years of friendship (and counting), and without whom I would be lost. To the gang in Montreal, Ottawa and Toronto, you are friends who are family, and you bring so much joy to my life.

To my Dad and Jill, thank you so much for being so excited at each stage; your encouragement means so much. Dan, Emily and sweet Finlay, love to you all.

Finally, Sofia, Sam and Emilia, you can't imagine how proud I am of you. Thank you for all the love you give. Pablo Samuel, eternal gratitude for your constant support and for encouraging me to make space for writing in my life. Without you, there would be no book, so it is also dedicated to you.

Notes and Translation from Spanish

A number of books and films assisted me in my research, and I gratefully acknowledge work by Marguerite Feitlowitz, Francisco Golman, Donald Hodges, Deborah Lee Norden, Luis Alberto Romero, Horacio Verbitsky, and Luis Puenzo.

While they are all fictional, some characters in this novel were touched and shaped by research. I do hope to have done justice in some small part to the bravery I encountered in those texts.

The following works are gratefully quoted: on page 5, lines from "Te nombraré veces y veces...," a poem by Juan Gelman; on page 45, a passage from "Twenty Thousand Leagues under the Sea," a novel by Jules Verne; on page 108, lines from "Balada para un loco," a song by Roberto Goyeneche; on page 68, reference to "Marie tu pleures," a song by Karkwa; on page 228, a line from "Mon pays," a song by Gilles Vigneault; on page 131, a line from a book by SARK; on page 139, lines from "Los Amigos," a poem by Julio Cortázar; on page 147, lines from "Street Haunting: A London Adventure (1930)," an essay by Virginia Woolf; on page 146, a line from "Poema XX," a poem by Pablo Neruda; on page 174, a reference to "El extraño del pelo largo," a song by La Joven Guardia; on pages 197 and 200, lines from "Poema 6," a poem by Pablo Neruda; on page 218, a reference to "Suzanne," a poem by Leonard Cohen; on page 231, a line from "Playa Girón," a song by Silvio Rodríguez.

Page 11

te nombraré veces y veces.
me acostaré con vos noche y día.
noches y días con vos.
me ensuciaré cogiendo con tu sombra.

I will name you time and time again.
I will sleep with you night and day.
Nights and days with you.
I will become dirty, fucking with your shadow.

Page 109

¡Loco! ¡Loco! ¡Loco!
Como un acróbata demente saltaré,
sobre el abismo de tu escote hasta sentir
que enloquecí tu corazón de libertad...
¡Ya vas a ver!

Madman! Madman! Madman!
Like a demented acrobat I will jump
over the abyss of your neckline until
I have crazed your heart of freedom
Soon you will see!

Page 135

Los amigos, en el tabaco, en el café, en el vino, al borde de la noche
se levantan, como esas voces que a lo lejos cantan, sin que se sepa
que, por el camino.

The friends, in tobacco, in coffee, in wine, on the edge of the
night they rise, like those voices that sing at a distance, who
knows what, along the way.

Page 161

Por cada obrero secuestrado, un patrón y un milico reventado.

For every kidnapped worker, a boss and a soldier blown up.

Translations, and any errors, are my own.

FSC
www.fsc.org

MIX
Paper
FSC® C100212

Printed by Imprimerie Gauvin
Gatineau, Québec